LOIS BI

I may be the head of the Prophesy County Sheriff's Department homicide unit, but I can't say I've seen all that many dead bodies. Though I guess I'd seen enough, 'cause I sure could tell the one in the car wasn't breathing. I opened the driver's door, half afraid Lois would fall out into my arms. But she didn't.

Her left arm dangled out as the door opened. I lifted the arm and felt for a pulse. It just seemed like the right thing to do. That's when I noticed the ignition key. It was in the "on" position. Looking up at the dashboard, I could see the needle of the gas gauge on "E" for empty. So now I knew what had killed Lois, although it had really been clear when I saw those cherry-pink faces. I knew now that Lois, probably in all innocence, had killed her family with that kitchen door that wasn't quite shut. I patted her hand and said, "I know you didn't mean to do it, honey. It was just one of those things."

Lois didn't reply.

——————————— ★ ———————————

"Ms. Cooper has a warm-hearted winner in Milt and the other droll residents of Prophesy County, Oklahoma." —*Dallas News*

"Susan Rogers Cooper is a gifted and perceptive writer whose characters are second to none!" —*Sharyn McCrumb*

Also available from Worldwide Mystery by
SUSAN ROGERS COOPER

HOUSTON IN THE REARVIEW MIRROR
THE MAN IN THE GREEN CHEVY

A Forthcoming Worldwide Mystery by
SUSAN ROGERS COOPER

CHASING AWAY THE DEVIL

OTHER PEOPLE'S HOUSES

SUSAN ROGERS COOPER

W🌐RLDWIDE.

TORONTO • NEW YORK • LONDON
AMSTERDAM • PARIS • SYDNEY • HAMBURG
STOCKHOLM • ATHENS • TOKYO • MILAN
MADRID • WARSAW • BUDAPEST • AUCKLAND

OTHER PEOPLE'S HOUSES

A Worldwide Mystery/January 1993

First published by St. Martin's Press Incorporated.

ISBN 0-373-26112-8

To Don and Evin, always
and
To Karen, Cindy, Michael and Howard

ONE

NOW, IN A BIG CITY, I suppose a peace officer going out on a homicide call and finding out it's somebody he knows is a bit of a shocker. In Prophesy County, the shocker is going out on a homicide call at all. The victim being somebody you know is just sort of a, if you'll excuse the expression, dead certainty.

When I got the call that there was a body over at 312 Grapevine Road, I knew by a quick look at the County Electric rollbooks that the body would have something to do with Lois Bell.

I'd seen Lois Bell every other Friday for the past year. She was the teller at the bank I traded at in Longbranch, the county seat of Prophesy County, the kind of person you know well enough to exchange pleasantries with. You know, like "Hey, Lois, hot enough for ya?"

"Hi, Milt. Sure is! How're you doing?"

"Fine, now that I got you to look at."

"I swear, you're the biggest flirt in Longbranch."

"I just try harder."

You know, pleasantries. She was a nice lady, though. Somewhere in her early thirties, medium height, medium-brown hair, medium pretty. I knew she was married because she wore a wedding ring, and I knew she had kids because there were pictures on her little shelf, although I never really paid that much attention to them. Or to her, if the truth be known. I guess if I'd thought about it, I would have had to say she and her family moved to town about a year ago, because I never saw her before that. In such a small community, I'd have noticed.

So when I got the call about a body at 312 Grapevine, I kinda winced, because that's what you do, and because this would be my second dead body in one day. And dead bodies are one thing I'm not real fond of. Never have been. That morning, two minutes after I'd walked into the station, Gladys, our clerk, had informed me she just got a call on a wreck out on Highway 5. As my day deputies, Dalton Petigrew and Mike Neils, were out on other calls, and as the sheriff is not one for going out on any call if there's somebody else to do it, I took it.

It had been a two-car collision, single drivers in each car. No passengers. Prophesy County is mostly farmland, with a lot of small farm roads and farmhouse driveways emptying into Highway 5. Tatum Ely, age eighty-five, was just pulling out of his driveway on his way to town when Terry Wilkes, age fifteen, was going past the driveway down Highway 5. Terry was going the speed limit, as it was only his third day behind the wheel on his own. He'd just gotten his license. Tatum slammed into the driver's side of Terry's little red Datsun with his great big Chevy two-ton truck. And I hadda go tell Terry's mom and dad. Not the best part of my job.

And I hadda give old Tatum a ticket, which he didn't understand. Course, Tatum didn't understand much of anything these days. The town he thought he was going into was Ardmore, not Longbranch, where he'd been headed. Tatum had lived in Ardmore as a young man. When I'd got the call about the body on Grapevine Road, I'd just gotten back from the judge's chambers, recommending they take Tatum Ely's license. This hadn't been my first recommendation on that count either. There was the time a couple of months ago when Tatum had run the red light just on the outskirts of Longbranch. He didn't hit anybody that time, but two cars coming the other direction with the light had hit end to end in trying to avoid old Tatum. Then of course there's been the time he'd parked his car halfway up the Lutheran Church steps. As it was a Thursday, there was nobody around for him to hit, but just the same. So far the judge hadn't found any of this to be worth pulling a man's freedom away from him, 'cause that's what a driver's license is when you live in the country. I'd hate to think the judge was prejudiced, but being as he was seventy-four years old himself, I wasn't sure he'd go along with my recommendation even now.

Course, I've got this theory. Ah, hell, it's more than a theory, it's an actual plan of action. All I need is to get somebody at state level to actually listen to me. My plan is this: Everybody has to take a driver's test every time they get their license renewed. Whaddaya think? See, this is my theory: Taking a driver's test to renew a license would take care of all them Tatum Elys out there, and there is a bunch of 'em, plus it could help with the drunken driver situation. Not the occasional drunken driver, but the pros. The ones that have been drinking steady since 1947. A real-life alcoholic is none too steady even sober, so the chances of them passing a driver's test are pretty slim. Even with people being on their best behavior, my plan would weed out a lot of potential traffic fatalities. So, call your local state rep and let's get this thing rolling, okay?

Anyway, I tried to push old Tatum from my mind and drove my unmarked squad car over to the house on Grapevine Road. I knew it was a rental because I happened to know the owner of this house, Clinton Austin, fella I went to school with. Owned about five rent houses in Longbranch. Clinton was considered a property holder of some standing in the community. The house was a nice little place, from the outside looked to be about a two bedroom, with connected garage. Lawn was trim for early autumn, everything looked tidy. Then I saw Dalton Petigrew standing on the front porch with a handkerchief over his nose and mouth.

"You call in the body, Dalton?" I asked.

"Hey, Milt. Yeah, Miz Kirby next door calls and says there's this real bad stench coming from here so could I come on by? Lordy, Milt, you ain't never seen nothing like this, I'm telling you."

I walked up to the door, expecting that sickly sweet odor you never get used to. The odor of death. It was there, all right, but barely noticeable under all the other smells.

"What the shit—" I started.

"Don't say shit, Milt, please, or I'll puke," Dalton said, still covering his mouth and nose.

I walked inside the front door, pulling my own handkerchief out of my back pocket and covering the lower half of my face. A man sat in a recliner chair staring glassy-eyed at a still-going TV set. He hadn't been seeing it for awhile, though. His face was a deep cherry pink, unnaturally so. Surrounding him were empty beer bottles, about a dozen of them, the one in his hand tilted slightly. Three cats at his feet grazed in the remnants of a pizza still in its stove box. The only furniture in the room was the recliner chair and an old sofa. A dirty diaper lay open on the sofa, flies thick around it. What looked like car parts lay in a heap in one corner of the room, and on the floor in front of the couch was a plate with half-eaten scrambled eggs, now dried out and brown. A few toys, most of them broken, were scattered around the floor.

As I walked through the living room, my shoes stuck occasionally to the carpet, it was that filthy. The kitchen was right beyond the recliner chair. I moved around the man and into the kitchen. Even with the handkerchief over my mouth and nose, it was heavy going. There was a great possibility, looking at that kitchen, that in the year the Bells had lived in the house, the garbage had never been taken out.

One of the sinks was backed up, with food and filthy water in it. A couple of roaches were doing the dead man's float in the mess. Food crusted the tabletop, what could be seen of it—the part that wasn't covered by garbage sitting next to partly full boxes of cereal and such. I slipped and almost lost my balance on something wet and slimy on the floor.

I backed out of the kitchen and started down the hall toward the bedrooms. The first bedroom was the kids' room. And they were all there. All three of them. The room held only a mattress without box springs, lying directly on the floor. All three children, a girl of about six or so, a boy who looked to have been about eight, and a baby had obviously been sleeping together on the mattress. All three children had died in their sleep, and all three little faces were that same deep, cherry-pink color. In a corner of the room were heaps of used diapers, and on the bed itself were wrappers from candy bars and bits of half-eaten snacks, sharing space with the soiled bed linens and dirty children's clothes. The clean clothes, or what I assumed to be clean, were all in a heap on the floor of the closet, which had no door.

The tears were rolling freely down my cheeks as I backed out of the babies' room and headed on down the hall. The master bedroom held a double bed and an old dresser. Heaps of dirty clothes lay next to heaps of clean, unironed clothes. There was no one there. The bathroom was across the hall from the kid's bedroom. The commode had overflowed and excrement was thick on the floor, along with used feminine pads, not even wrapped in toilet paper or anything. I didn't step into the bathroom. If Lois was standing in the bathtub behind the mildewed shower curtain with a butcher knife at the ready, I guessed I'd never know.

Dalton, the coward, was still out on the porch. "Any sign of the wife?" I called to him.

"Ain't seen her, Milt."

"Well, go next door to Miz Kirby's and use her phone. Call the bank and ask for Miz Bell. If she's there, tell her who you are and tell her to come on home. If she's not there, just say thank you and hang up. Don't tell nobody who you are."

"Yeah, Milt, okay, I'll do that."

The thing with Dalton is you gotta spell things out.

I turned back around and surveyed the living room again. That's when I noticed the door against the left-hand wall, right before the entryway to the kitchen. I figured that led to the garage. I walked past the dead man I presumed to be Mr. Bell and opened the door. Or pushed it open wider—the latch didn't work and the door hadn't really been closed. A 1978 Ford station wagon, maroon with rust, sat in the small garage. And Lois Bell sat in the car.

I may be the head of the Prophesy County Sheriff's Department homicide unit, but I can't say I've seen all that many dead bodies. Though I guess I'd seen enough, 'cause I sure could tell the one in the car wasn't breathing. I opened the driver's door, half afraid Lois would fall out into my arms. But she didn't. She just lay there, her head back against the headrest, her face that same old color, cherry pink, her right arm on the bucket seat next to her, her left arm dangling out as the door opened. Her arms and hands were a paler shade of that pink color.

I lifted the arm that hung out of the car and felt for a pulse. It just seemed like the right thing to do. That's when I noticed the ignition key. It was in the "on" position. Looking up at the dashboard, I could see the needle of the gas gauge on "E" for empty. So now I knew what had killed Lois, although it had really been clear when I saw those cherry-pink faces. I knew now that Lois, probably in all innocence, had killed her family with that kitchen door that wasn't quite shut. I patted her hand and said, "I know you didn't mean to do it, honey. It was just one of those things." Lois didn't reply.

Floyd Ackerman's hearse showed up about the same time Dalton got back from Mrs. Kirby's house. "Milt? Hey, Milt, you in there?" I heard Dalton call from the front door.

"Out in the garage, Dalton. Go through the living room. Door by the kitchen."

He made it. "Miz Bell wasn't at work, Milt."

"Guess not, Dalton. She's right here."

"Oh." He stuck his head into the car. "She dead?"

"Far as I can tell. Course, Dr. Jim's gonna have to declare her dead."

"What the hell happened, Milt? They ain't been shot, or stabbed or nothing. A virus, maybe?"

"You been watching *Outer Limits* reruns again, Dalton? Look at the key there." I pointed toward the ignition.

"Okay." Dalton looked. "Okay?"

"What do you see?"

"Whaddaya mean?"

"What do you see?"

He looked around the body again at the key. "Well, I dunno, Milt. I guess I see a key."

"What position is it in?"

Again, he looked around the body at the key. "Looks like it's on, Milt."

He straightened up. "But the motor ain't running."

"Look at the gas gauge," I said. I wasn't sure why I was playing this game with Dalton. I guess it beat dealing with reality.

"It's on empty!" He smiled real big. Then he frowned. "What does that mean?"

I sighed. "I reckon they died of carbon monoxide poisoning. Miz Bell came out here and started the car and sat in it. The poison leaked around the bad door frame to the house, went into the house, and got the rest of the family. The car ran all night and emptied the tank. Musta happened awhile ago or we'd smell the exhaust fumes. And the color of the skin? See that on Miz Bell? That pinkish color? That's a sure sign. The husband and kids got it too. So, it was carbon monoxide poisoning. That's the way I figure it."

"Geez, Milt, that's plumb awful."

"Ain't it, though? Only thing I can't figure is them cats. How come they're not dead?"

"Well, the front door was ajar when I got here, Milt. You reckon they got in after the stuff kinda wore off?"

"Must be."

We stood together for awhile in the garage and stared at Lois Bell and thought about the awfulness of it all. Then Floyd Ackerman's grandson Bobby Lee came to the door of the garage and said, between popping his gum, "You ready for me to take these stiffs away, Mr. Kovak?"

"Not yet, Bobby Lee. Dr. Jim's gotta look at 'em first. Declare 'em dead."

"Well, shit, I can do that." He pointed a bony finger at Lois Bell and said, "You're dead!" then giggled like hell. That's when I figured Floyd and his boy Marvis might have a problem when it got time to pass the funeral home on down to this generation.

"You go on out now and wait. Let me know when you see Dr. Jim's car coming."

"Sure thing, Mr. Kovak." He left, humming and popping his gum. From the living room, I heard him shout, "Dr. Jim's here!" just as the man himself stuck his head out the door from the living room to the garage, followed by Charlie Budrock, his new assistant.

"God's sake, Milt, what'd you get me into this time?" Dr. Jim asked.

"Well, seems we got bodies all over the damn place."

"Seen the one in the living room. He's dead. Got one here, huh?"

Dr. Jim came over to the car and made a cursory exam of Lois Bell. "She's dead. What else you got?"

"Three little kids in one of the bedrooms."

"Ah, shit."

I led him on back to the kids' bedroom where he checked them over and declared them all dead. I stole a look at the assistant, who hadn't said a word but was looking pretty green around the gills.

"Looks like carbon monoxide poisoning to me," I said.

"Yeah? Where'd you get your medical degree?"

"All I'm saying is the car's ignition was in the 'on' position, the gas tank's empty, and they all got this bright-pink tinge to their skin. 'Cept I can't see how it got to the whole family."

"No problem," said Charlie Budrock. Charlie'd just graduated OU with his engineering degree and was working part time for Dr. Jim waiting for his entrance to the real world, somewhere other than Prophesy County. Pulling a calculator out of his pocket, he poked it a few times and said, "Shit, no problem." He pointed at the car Lois was still in. "A car that old with a V-eight engine burning, say, eighteen to twenty gallons of leaded gas would produce twice the amount of shit you need to kill everybody in a house this size." He put the calculator back in his pocket and grinned real big at Dr. Jim and me.

"Well, why don't we just wait and see what the autopsy report shows?" Dr. Jim said to me. "Meanwhile, why don't you go find the next a' kin or something?"

"I don't tell you how to do your job, you don't tell me how to do mine. Right?" I asked.

"Right."

Touchy old bastard. By now my nose had gotten used to the stink, so I set about looking for the family records. I found Lois's purse in the backseat of the car. Driver's license, social security card, pictures of her kids, and three one-dollar bills. Her husband's wallet, in his back pants pocket, showed the same, except he had a fiver and some change. In the bedroom, in a drawer that had obviously been Lois's, because of the panties and such sharing the space, I found a checkbook and some receipts and other such. Every record was less than a year old, every receipt was for a place in Longbranch.

Nowhere in that house, amid all that filth and squalor, did I find a letter, a postcard, birthday cards, anything like that. The bills I found in a kitchen drawer were all up to date and all for the Longbranch area, all utility bills and one charge bill from the drugstore. No national credit cards, not even a Sears. There were no birth certificates, insurance papers, or anything of the such. Then I remembered Lois worked at a bank. A safe deposit box.

I drove into town to the Longbranch Savings and Loan and went in, asking to see Dwayne Dickey, the president, on Sheriff's department business. Dwayne Dickey wasn't exactly a friend of mine. He'd been dating my ex-wife and there was a rumor going on around town that he planned on marrying her. Maybe I shoulda been grateful. I wasn't.

"Well, hey, Milt!" He came out of his office, all hail-fellow-good-cheer, pumping my hand up and down like the long-lost buddy he wasn't.

"Dwayne, how you doing?"

"Great, just great!" He coulda said fine. Most people just say fine. "How are you?" He patted me on the back as he said this, squeezing one of my shoulders as he did. It took a lot of control not to elbow him in the gut.

"Personally, Dwayne, I'm great. Just great. But professionally, I got a problem. Can we go in your office?"

"Why sure, Milt. Nelda," he called to the lady who'd gone to get him in the first place, "get us some coffee. How you take yours, Milt? Nelda, make mine black."

"Black's fine with me," I said. I preferred cream and sugar, but somehow that didn't seem manly enough at the moment.

We went into his office and got ourselves settled in our chairs, him in a big, black leather desk chair, me in a little black visitor's chair, and waited while Nelda served us our coffee and left, closing the door behind her.

"So, Milt, what can I do for you? No problem with LaDonna, I hope?"

LaDonna was my ex-wife. I had to hope, before she married this guy, she'd take into consideration how ridiculous her new name would be. LaDonna

Kovak was kinda pretty. LaDonna Dickey was something else entirely.

"No, nothing like that. It's about one of your tellers. Lois Bell."

"Well, Lois isn't here today, Milt."

"I know that, Dwayne. Lois is dead."

For a split second I saw what Dwayne Dickey really looked like, without all the false cheeriness and the calculated facial expressions. Then he fell into his shocked isn't-that-awful, tsk-tsk look. "Heavens to Betsy, Milt! What happened?"

When was the last time you heard someone say "Heavens to Betsy"? Not nearly long enough, huh? So anyway, I told him. Sorta.

"The whole family? The children?" He shook his head several times. "What in the world caused it, Milt?"

"We're not sure yet. Coroner's looking into it. Meanwhile, I gotta notify the next of kin before the paper gets wind of this. If I could look at her job application and see who she has down there for emergency contact and such, that'd help. And, oh, by the by"—real casual like—"she did have a safe-deposit box here, didn't she?"

"I don't know offhand, Milt, but if she did, you'd have to have a court order to get into it."

"Well, the job application then?"

He turned to the phone, punched a couple of intercom numbers, and said, "Mary Anne? This is Mr.

Dickey. Bring me the personnel file on Lois Bell. Thank you, honey." He hung up the phone and looked toward the door. I turned and looked too. It took less than a minute for Mary Anne to walk from her desk a yard away to the door and hand Dwayne the file. "Thank you, hon," he said, smiling that sharklike smile of his.

He flipped through the pages and stopped near the back, reading. "Well, says here next a' kin is her husband, Bill."

"Case of emergency?"

"Her husband, Bill."

"Where'd they move here from, Dwayne?"

He read a bit. "Doesn't say, Milt."

"She have any other jobs? What's her résumé look like?"

"This was her first job."

"Oh."

"But the funniest thing...."

"What's that?"

He thought for a moment. "Well, nothing I can put my finger on. But... well, I interviewed her myself. I remember that now. Her saying this would be her first job and all. Been raising her kids. But, when she started working, seemed to me she'd done this kinda thing before."

"What do you mean?"

"Well...I can't rightly say. But, you know, Milt...she just knew things that maybe she shouldn't a' known if she'd never worked before.... Hell, if she'd never worked in a bank before. Little stuff you wouldn't understand.''

Did I mention I didn't like this guy? ''Anything else in that file that can tell me anything?'' I knew he'd rather die a harelip than turn that file over to me to let me look for myself. I decided that court order I was gonna get for Lois's safe deposit box might just mention her personnel file while I was about it. And maybe Dwayne's desk.

''No... nothing worth mentioning.'' He smiled. ''Sorry.''

I stood up. ''Well, thank you kindly for all your help, Dwayne,'' I said, holding out my hand to shake his. We stood there for a few seconds, each showing the other how childish we were by squeezing each other's hand and waiting for the other to yell uncle. It was a draw.

Outside the bank I passed a lady on her way in, hauling two little kids behind her. The little boy, about three or such, was crying his eyes out. ''I was sleeping! Let me sleep, Mama!''

''I'm not leaving you in the car, young man!''

''I was sleeping! You woke me up!''

''Hush, now. They'll give you a lollipop in the bank if you're a good boy.''

''I don't wanna lollipop! I wanna sleep!''

His big sister, who looked to be about five, bounced around her mother and brother, circling them again and again, chanting "Bobby is a sissy! Bobby is a sissy!"

"Hush, Margaret," Mama said. "Stop it now!"

I watched this little dramette and wondered. Yesterday this lady would've been just another person, just another normal, all-American mother of two, dragging her kids into the bank. Today I had to wonder. I had to wonder what was going on in her house, behind her closed doors. Lois Bell had been just another mother with three kids and a husband and a job at the bank. A nice lady, like this one, neatly dressed, hair in place, not too much makeup but not none at all either. It didn't seem fair that I knew Lois's secrets. That I knew she had been losing it for a lot longer than anyone could have known. How could she have lived like that? How could she have raised kids like that?

And here I was, having my dirty underwear laundered by my sister, judging her. Somehow, that wasn't fair. But like my old daddy used to say, "Don't believe nobody that tells you life's fair. They're either a con artist or a used car salesman."

TWO

My SISTER LIVES with me. I don't live with my sister. I bought a house about a year and a half ago up on Mountain Falls Road, about eighteen miles from work. Then my sister got herself widowed down in Houston last winter and I moved her and her three kids up here to live with me. Before they moved in, I had two rooms of furniture for my nine-room house. Now we got furniture to spare. And I have absolutely no privacy.

My sister, her name's Jewel Anne Hotchkiss, and we hardly spoke to each other for the first thirty years of our lives. Now she's making up for lost time. She's a bigger nag than my ex-wife ever was.

"Milton, I swear to God, you're the sloppiest man I've ever seen!" "Milton, if you're not gonna make it for dinner, at least have the decency to call!" "Milton, watch your language in front of my children!" "Milton, that cat of yours is shedding all over the sofa!" And on and on and on.

And then there's the fact that the kids insist on watching their TV shows so I can't watch mine. And there's the fact that my sister could use a cookbook to boil water. And there's the fact that her oldest son,

Leonard, who's seventeen, is a pain in the neck. Always bitching about living in the sticks. And there's the fact that I share a bathroom with the two youngest, one of whom's a girl who isn't real neat when it comes to putting away her makeup, leaves her blow dryer plugged in, and spends entirely too much time in there altogether. Other than those few things, I guess we're getting along fine.

That is, as long as I try not to remember the other fact. The fact about how Glenda Sue Robertson hasn't spent a night in my house since the troops moved in. When we're together, it's at her place, a little bitty old house trailer on a mangy piece of land she got in her divorce settlement from my used-to-be-best-friend, Linn Robertson.

I hate going to that trailer for a number of reasons. One, it's so tiny I have to stand in the hall and aim at the little john when I'm in a mind to take a leak. Two, Glenda Sue collects cacti. All sorts. And they're all over the damn place. I've sat on a couple over the years. It's not a pleasant experience. Three, whenever I drive up to that little bitty old house trailer, I'm reminded of the many times I drove up there in my squad car when I was first on the force to drag my old buddy Linn off his wife. And reminded of the times I'd called an ambulance to have the paramedics look at the lady's numerous injuries. I guess that place must not have had the same memories for Glenda Sue. Or if it did, she stayed there for some reason only a shrink could fathom.

But that night, the night after the day when Lois Bell et al were discovered, I didn't have to think about Glenda Sue's house trailer because it was a Tuesday. Glenda Sue and I only saw each other on Wednesdays, Fridays, and an occasional Sunday. So instead I went home to the troops.

I walked in the front door and from the foyer could see everybody in the living room, couch pillows on the floor, rug rolled up in a corner, knick-knacks in a box on the floor, cleaning equipment spread hither and yon.

"Marlene! I saw you shove that trash under the pillow! Get it out! Now!" Jewel hollered from her general's vantage point three steps up the staircase. "And you, Leonard, I told you to wash out that fireplace! Not just brush it out! First you brush it out, then you get a scrub brush and some Mr. Clean and clean it! I don't care if you have to stick your whole body in there, you clean it!"

"Hey, ya'll," I called quietly from the doorway. "I'm home."

All three kids rushed at me like it was what they usually did. It wasn't.

"Hey, Uncle Milt! Boy, I'm glad you're home!" Carl, the youngest, said.

"Bring me anything?" Marlene chirped. Why, I don't know. I never had before.

"So, hey, Uncle Milt. How's everything at the sheriff's office?" Leonard asked. He'd never asked that before.

"What's going on?" I ventured.

Jewel limped her way over to the doorway. "You three! Get your butts back to work!" The kids moved with slumping shoulders and long faces back to their assigned tasks. "And you!" She pointed a finger at me. "I want you upstairs and I want that room of yours cleaned."

"Now wait just a goddamn minute!"

"I mean it! Somebody comes in here in the middle of the night, kills us all—you want the newspaper taking pictures of your filthy room?"

I walked to the hall table where the afternoon paper—the only paper in Longbranch—rested. There on the front page was a photo of Lois Bell's kitchen. Light was beginning to dawn.

"You maybe overreacting a trifle, Miz Jewel?" I asked, tossing the paper back on the table. An advertising circular slid out and fell to the floor. Jewel Anne pounced on it like it was a tree roach sneaking in.

"I knew her!" she wailed.

"Yes, ma'am, so did I."

"What happened?"

"I can't talk about an active investigation."

"Bullshit."

That took me aback. Jewel Anne doesn't cuss. Mama told her once it wasn't ladylike. "Far as I can tell so far, nobody snuck in in the middle of the night and done 'em all in. If that's what you're thinking. It looks right now like suicide and accident."

The kids had moved to the living room doorway. Jewel turned on them. "You get back in there and clean!"

On any given day we could entertain the Pope, if we were Catholic, without a moment's notice. You could drop a baby in the toilet and not worry about it getting any infections, only drowning. If you sat for any length of time in one place, you had to worry about having a doily spread out on your lap. That's the way Jewel Anne kept house. She was a fanatic. Course, right now, I guess she didn't have a lot else to put her mind to.

"This house is clean, Jewel. And nobody's dying here. Nobody's taking any pictures."

"You can't be too careful," she said, and stormed back into the living room.

Tact being the better part of valor and all, I quietly stole up to my room on the second floor. My room on the second floor was an addition built by one of the house's many previous owners that went the width of the house and was all windows except for one tiny wall that hooked on to one of the original upstairs bedrooms. From the windows I could look out on twin peaks of what we call mountains in

Oklahoma and the little valley in between that was in another county. It was a great view. When storms blew in from the north, it was an even greater view. There was a time, before I owned the house, when I stood at one of those windows with a lady... but, hell, I'm not gonna go into that. Memories are memories, and best kept for late at night when you can do something about them.

I looked around my humble domicile and wondered what in the hell Jewel had been talking about. The room was clean. Sheets on the bed were less than a week old, the pile of clothes in the corner were my after-work clothes, which I was just gonna put on now anyway. So there were a couple of peanut shells on the rug from last night's midnight munchies, and a couple of wadded-up Kleenexes on the nightstand from when I had that cold last month. That's not filth. It's just mess. There's a difference.

I walked to the nightstand and picked up the Kleenexes and tossed them in the wastebasket next to the table. Then I sat down on the bed and thought about Lois Bell.

Why? That was the big unanswered question, unanswered because there was no suicide note found. Which bothered me. In my experience as chief of homicide, I knew there was usually a note. Not that I'd ever had a suicide before, but I read up on these things. Suicides generally leave notes. That's what my journals say. Course, it's not a hard and fast rule,

God's not gonna send 'em back if they forget to leave one, but the rule of thumb is: Suicides usually leave notes. Lois Bell didn't.

Thinking about Lois, I came up with the few facts I knew. Lois and her husband, Bill, moved to Prophesy County about a year ago from place unknown. No records in the house to indicate where they moved from. Check the safe deposit box. Get Judge Rodgers to issue a court order in the morning. Okay. Go through the house more thoroughly. I didn't want to do that. Get Dalton to do it. Chicken shit. I'll do it. Okay. Talk to her co-workers about any recent problems she might have talked about. Or ask if they'd seen any changes in her over the past few weeks. More depressed, etc. Okay. What else? Take my bath and get in bed before Jewel Anne comes up with anything else for me to do. Okay.

THE NEXT MORNING I was in Judge Rodgers's office at the crack of 9 A.M. He showed up around nine-thirty and signed a court order allowing me access to the safe deposit box. I didn't ask for the personnel file. He wasn't in that great a mood. I got to the bank about the time the guard unlocked the door and handed Dwayne the court order. He smiled and handed it to a flunky who took me down the stairs to the basement where the vault and safe deposit boxes were. I went into one of the little rooms they have that give you instant claustrophobia and opened the box.

On top was a legal-length black binder tied with a red ribbon. Inside were birth certificates. Lois Anne Bell, née Malroohney, born in Americus, Georgia, April 9, 1952. William Alexander Bell, born in Atlanta, Georgia, September 14, 1950. William Alexander Bell, Jr., born in Shreveport, Louisiana, December 11, 1979. Melissa Diane Bell, born in Shreveport, Louisiana, June 23, 1982. And Anna Marie Bell, born in Oklahoma City, Oklahoma, August 1, 1986. Also in the black binder were high school graduation certificates. Lois Anne Malroohney, class of '71, Martin Luther King, Jr. High School, Americus, Georgia. William Alexander Bell, class of '68, Jefferson Davis High School, Atlanta, Georgia. And a marriage certificate, dated October 12, 1971, signed by a JP in Albany, Georgia. Army discharge papers for William Alexander Bell, honorably discharged in August 1971, at the rank of corporal, was the last thing in the black binder.

I put everything back in and put the binder aside to take with me. Under that in the safe deposit box was a small jewelry box. Inside sat a gold brooch, designed in the shape of a seagull with a diamond chip in its one eye. I picked up the brooch to get a better look. When I did, the cotton it rested on stuck to the pin and came up with it. Under the cotton was a set of captain's bars. Grandma's brooch and

Grandpa's captain's bars? I set them on the other side of the box. The binder was one pile, the pile that went with me, the jewelry box another pile, the pile that went back in.

The next item was an eight-and-a-half by eleven-inch manila envelope, with "1986 Income Tax" scrawled across the top. Inside were all the papers one accumulates for Uncle Sam. W2s, receipts, etc. I picked up the W2s and noticed Lois Bell had lied to Dwayne Dickey. Not a criminal offense and understandable, given my own bent about Dwayne Dickey. Lois Bell had held a job before, at a credit union, namely the Oklahoma Civic Workers Federal Credit Union in Oklahoma City. She made $14,942.35 in 1986. Husband Bill had contributed $11,312.72 in his capacity as mechanic at a Goodyear outlet on Columbus Street in Oklahoma City. And the baby had cost them $712.93 after insurance. All in all, after insurance, they had spent a total of $1,438 (in round numbers) on medical bills. And $168 (in round numbers) on interest on various charge cards they no longer possessed. Child care had come to a whopping, $3,380. They didn't own a house. The address listed was in Oklahoma City. I put that on the take-with-me pile.

The next items, which were in the stay pile, were obvious Mother's Day gifts—an ashtray made out of clay in the shape of a child's hand, a picture frame made out of Popsicle sticks, and a small macrame wall-hanging that was done either by one of the kids or by somebody under intense physical and mental therapy. At the bottom was a small purple velvet drawstring bag. Inside the bag were two wedding rings and an engagement ring. The engagement ring had a really nice diamond, at least a carat, and the bands, a small one belonging to a woman, the other larger, for a man's hand, were both heavy gold. Engraved inside the lady's ring was "DT to AJ, AML"; inside the man's, "AJ to DT, Forever."

There was nothing anywhere indicating next of kin. I put the "stay" stuff back in, stuck the "keep" stuff under my arm, gave the box back to the attendant, and headed back up the stairs to interview Lois Bell's co-workers.

Lois had been one of three tellers, stationed in the middle booth. On the left side of her was the head teller, a lady named Bernice Wiggins, who'd worked at the bank longer than anybody still living. The woman was *old*. On the other side was a young man I barely recognized. It took me a minute to realize it was Junior Dickey, son of my nemesis. I stuck my head in Dwayne's door, hoping I was bothering him.

"I need to speak to the two tellers who worked with Lois, Dwayne. Can you find me some quiet place I can interview them?"

As usual, he delegated his authority, and his secretary showed me to the break room, empty at this hour. "I'll have to arrange subs for them but I'll do that as quickly as possible. It's bad enough only having two tellers now."

In my head, I chastised Lois Bell for her thoughtlessness at leaving the bank shorthanded. After about ten minutes, Bernice Wiggins knocked on the door and entered.

I stood up and held out my hand. Mrs. Wiggins took it like it was dipped in cow shit and quickly let it go. "Please sit down, Miz Wiggins," I said.

She sat and looked at me. No expression. Just looked at me. "I was hoping you could answer some questions about Lois Bell," I said.

"Probably not."

"Pardon?"

"I said probably not."

"Well, you worked right next to her for over a year, isn't that right?"

"Yes."

"So, you two ever talk?"

"No."

"Not ever?"

"Hardly ever."

"So you did talk some?"

"Not really."

I was trying real hard not to let my exasperation show. "You know what her husband's name was?" I asked.

"Bill."

"What about her kids?"

"Billy, Melissa, and the baby, Anna Marie."

"Well, see, now, you must have done some talking."

"Not really."

"Had she changed much lately?"

"No."

"I mean, did she seem depressed, despondent, anything like that?"

"Not that I noticed."

And that was about as much as I got out of her. Although it took me ten more minutes to find that out. A few minutes after she left, there was a tentative knock on the door. As it wasn't followed immediately by someone's entrance, I called, "Come on in." The only response to that was another tentative knock. I had to wonder if maybe Mrs. Wiggins had locked the door behind her, but when I got up and went to the door, I noticed it wasn't even latched. I opened it and saw Junior Dickey standing there.

Now, I had a natural affinity to Junior Dickey. You just had to admire a guy who could disappoint his father as much as Junior had. A quick calculation put Junior in my mind as just over eighteen years old, and in all those eighteen years, he hadn't done one damn thing his daddy could brag on.

I think Dwayne and his cronies probably figured Junior was gay, mainly because when it came to pretty, Junior Dickey couldda run for homecoming queen. And to top it all off, he was just plain smart. Him and another guy single-handedly started the chess club at school and managed actually to get into competition. But since both of 'em graduated that past spring, I hear the chess club at the Longbranch High School is no longer. But he didn't play football. He didn't play baseball. And he didn't play basketball. So, naturally, as a son to Dwayne Dickey, he was a failure.

I said, "Hey, Junior, how you doing?" and ushered him in.

"Just fine, Mr. Kovak, how are you?"

"Fine, come on and sit down."

We found some chairs and sat, him with his shoulders hunched and me looking official as all hell.

"I need to ask you some questions about Miz Bell," I said.

"Yes, sir."

"You two ever talk much?"

"Sometimes."

"She seemed depressed lately?"

"No."

"You didn't notice anything different about her, say, in the last couple of weeks?"

"No."

"She ever talk about her family?"

"No."

"What did you talk about?"

He shrugged his shoulders. "Nothing much. Books mostly."

"She do a lot of reading?"

"No."

"Then how come you talked about books?"

"I read a lot. She liked to hear about the books I was reading."

"Oh, I see." Of course, I didn't. What did he do, sit there on his high teller's stool and recite "The Boy Stood on the Burning Deck" or what? "That's all ya'll talked about?"

"You know, just stuff."

"Yeah, like what stuff?"

"You know, what was on TV the night before, stuff like that."

"Oh. Well. I guess that'll do it, Junior. Thank you for your time."

Junior nodded his head and stood up to leave. As he headed for the door, I asked him, "How come you're not at college? I figured you for going to OU."

"I'm starting the spring semester. But not at OU. I'll be heading to Houston. Rice University."

"Well, that's great. I hear that's a tough school to get into."

For the first time since he'd come in the room, he smiled. A sorrowful, pitiful smile, but a smile nonetheless. "Yeah, even the jocks have brains. Sorta."

I laughed and he left. I questioned a few more employees, but none of them knew much, if anything, about Lois Bell. Finally I left for the station.

Once there, I stuck my head in the sheriff's office door and asked, "Sheriff, got a minute?"

He looked up from the papers on his desk. "Sure, Milton. Rest your ass."

I put the stuff from the safe deposit box on his desk and sat down in one of the two visitors' chairs. My office only gets one. Course, the lesser deputies get only half a chair. That's a joke.

"Got something on the Bell thing?" Elberry asked. Elberry Blankenship is the sheriff of Prophesy County and has been longer than either he or I would like to think about. He's a good man. Mean as a junkyard dog, but a good man.

"Can't find the next of kin."

"How come?"

"Well, because it's not there. Looked around in the house, got a court order and went through the safe deposit box. Can't find nothing. 'Cept a lot of confusion."

"What sort of confusion?"

"Bill, the husband, had discharge papers in there says he was discharged a corporal. But there's a pair of captain's bars in there. And some wedding rings with the wrong initials on 'em."

"So the captain's bars belonged to his daddy. The wedding rings to her mama or whatever."

"Yeah. I thought about that. But the wedding rings—the initials don't even match up to her maiden name."

"So they were her maternal grandma's."

"Okay."

"They ever go to a doctor here in Longbranch? Doctor would maybe have some next of kin on the papers they filled out."

"I don't know if they ever went to a doctor here or not."

"Well, hell, Milton, we ain't got that many doctors in Prophesy County. Call 'em."

So I went back to my office and got out the phone book and started dialing and got the same rigmarole every time. "We can't give out that information." "The patient is deceased." "Which one?" "All of 'em." "Oh. That's awful. Just a minute . . . no record." So then I called the Longbranch Memorial Hospital. After the same bullshit, I finally got somebody who admitted that William Bell, Jr., had been admitted to the emergency room three months previously. But there was no new information on the papers filled out by his mother. I figured my next calls would have to be long-distance ones to Oklahoma City. I hoped the county commissioners wouldn't shit little green apples when they saw the bill.

But before I got a chance to start running up the county telephone bill, I got a call from Dr. Jim. "Carbon monoxide poisoning."

I didn't say a word.

"You hear me?"

"Yes, sir, I surely did. Carbon monoxide poisoning."

"Just like I figured when I first saw 'em," Dr. Jim said.

"Right."

"The old man was drunk as a skunk by the amount of booze in him. And the lady had a nasty crack on her head."

"What do you mean?"

"What do you mean what do I mean? She had a crack on the head. Hit her head on something."

I felt those old icy fingers going up and down my spine. "Like maybe a fatal crack on the head?"

"Shit, no. She wouldn't have been that cherry-pink color we both saw if she'd died from the head injury. She died of carbon monoxide poisoning, same as the rest of them."

"What caused the head injury?"

"Shit if I know."

"Can you tell how old the injury is?"

I could almost hear the good doctor's shrug over the phone. "No more than twelve to twenty-four hours before death, by the look and feel of the thing."

"Would it have caused unconsciousness?"

"Maybe. Maybe not."

I thought for a minute, then asked, "Anything else? Distinguishing marks, et cetera?"

"Still haven't found the next of kin, huh?"

"No, sir."

"Well, she had the usual stretch marks. And a C-section scar. Looked to be fairly new. Probably the last baby. Now the husband—nothing interesting, 'cept if you get off to beer guts and tattoos."

"Tattoos?"

"Actually, tattoo. Only one. 'Semper Fi.' Almost missed it. It's inside the crack of his ass."

"Ouch. Semper Fi, huh? As in a few good men?"

"Yeah."

"Well, that's mighty interesting."

"Why's that?"

"Because his discharge papers show he was in the army—not the marines."

"I'm all aquiver."

"Well, I think it's interesting."

"He had a hernia operation about three to five years ago, by the scar tissue. That turn you on?"

"Just gives me more places to look."

"Always nice to see a man happy in his work."

"Dr. Jim, if you were a woman I'd swear you were on the rag."

"Milton, if I was a woman, I'd turn you in to the sheriff for a sexist remark like that."

"Good thing you're not a woman."

"That's what my wife's always claimed. Bye."

I sat back and thought about what I had. Okay, maybe I read too many mystery novels. But something was wrong here. I didn't like a corporal in the army being in possession of captain's bars and having a marine tattoo up his ass. I also didn't like that crack on Lois Bell's head. But she and her whole family died of carbon monoxide poisoning. If the truth be known, I didn't like one blasted thing about this case. I didn't like the fact that Lois Bell lived in secret filth while the world saw her as a normal, neat lady.

But most of all, I didn't like that crack on her head. I didn't like that one goddamn bit. But for want of anything better to do, I decided to go interview the neighbors.

Mrs. Kathy Anne Hope lived on one side of the little two-bedroom where the Bells had died. Her baby-sitter said she didn't get home from her job as a dental technician for Dr. Michaels until around six. So I went to see Mrs. Kirby, the neighbor who'd originally turned in the call.

I rang the doorbell once and waited. I knew Mrs. Kirby used a walker so I saw no need to ring the bell more than once. After about two minutes, the door opened.

"Hey, Miz Kirby," I greeted her, with a smile. She'd been my Sunday school teacher when I'd been in junior high. Always a nice lady, never quick to judge other people because they didn't believe like her. I remembered once back in those days when she'd jumped straddle a friend of mine who'd said some disparaging remarks about a new kid in school who was a Catholic, and Mexican to boot. She'd said something then that'd stuck in my mind all these years: "Learn from him. People of different cultures, different beliefs, have something to teach you. Something that can help strengthen your own faith. Find out what it is." I'd never told anybody about how that impressed me, figuring being impressed by anything a Sunday school teacher had to say was a little corny. But I'd remembered it.

"Hey yourself, Chief Deputy," she greeted.

"Mind if I come in and talk a bit about the Bells?"

She shook her head, not in denial but sorrow, and opened the door wider. "The damnedest thing's ever happened to people I know! Come on in. You want some coffee?"

"Don't go to any trouble...."

"There's been a pot of coffee brewing in this house steady since the day I got married and moved in here. No trouble, Chief Deputy."

I stood in the living room and waited while she made her slow, painful way to the kitchen and back. I didn't offer to help. I figured that'd be more painful than moving around. After we got our coffee and were sitting down, I asked her, "What can you tell me about the Bells? You know of any next of kin?"

"Milton, I can't tell you nothing about those people. They lived next door there for a good year, I suppose, but I can't say I spoke more than a couple of words with the mother. Now the two older kids, they'd come over now and again for cookies and to play with Rex." At the mention of his name, an Appaloosa-spotted dog got up from his bed by the fireplace and moved over to flop his head on Mrs. Kirby's feet. "But, no, Milton, I can't say I can tell you anything about 'em. Never saw nobody come visit, not that I kept my eye to the window peeking. Not my style."

"Did Mr. Bell work?"

"Oh, for a while. Over at the Gulf station on the highway to Tulsa. The only way I know that is my sister Maybelle and me stopped there one time on our way to Tulsa to see her daughter. But then about four, maybe five months ago, I noticed his truck was at the house all the time during the day. So I figured he got laid off or something. But she worked at the bank...."

"Yes, ma'am."

"You know, it's the funniest thing...but she used to be real friendly to me at the bank. Saying 'Hey, Miz Kirby' whenever she saw me. Asking after my health. But I walk out in the yard same time as her, she wouldn't even answer my hidy."

"Yes, ma'am, that is strange."

"But, Lord, Milton, when I saw the inside of that house I nearly died! I never been a big believer in the cleanliness-is-next-to-Godliness stuff—I figure a body's got a dollar, better spent on a can of beans than a bar of soap—but that house! Milton...that house was just plain evil. It was like the Devil himself was housed in that filth! And those babies—dear Lord...."

"Yes, ma'am. I know." I stood up. "Thank you for the coffee and the information, Miz Kirby. I best get on with this investigation. I'll go on up to that Gulf station, see what I can find out."

"Sorry I couldn't be of more help."

I shook her brittle hand lightly and left to get in my car and head up the Tulsa highway.

THREE

I DROVE UP the Tulsa highway with the windows of the squad car rolled down, letting the cool autumn breeze ruffle what's left of my hair. The Millerby Gulf Station had easy access off the highway and looked to be doing a steady trade. It was a new station, with those modern pumps only a rocket scientist can work. Four big bays jutted out from the side of the office, and two guys lounged by the open doors of the bays. The steady trade all appeared to be at the gas pumps. No cars were in the bays or hoisted up.

I parked the squad car and got out and introduced myself. Not that it did me a hell of a lot of good. They were willing enough to answer my questions, but they weren't even sure if Bill Bell was married. Much less who his next of kin was.

By the time I got through with them, it was quitting time, so I took the unmarked squad car back to the mostly empty parking lot of the sheriff's department and exchanged it for my '55. That's my personal car. A 1955 Chevy Bel Air hardtop. Cherry. My ex-wife never asked me to choose between it and her.

If she had, we'd have been divorced a lot sooner. I love my '55.

Wednesdays were my usual nights to be with Glenda Sue, but this Wednesday she'd agreed to work for a friend whose daughter was having a baby shower. So instead of heading as per my usual to the little trailer, I headed instead toward Mountain Falls Road.

I made the eighteen miles home in record time, worrying all the way about what Jewel might have fixed for dinner. Since Jewel moved in, I've noticed myself longing for Lean Cuisine. I couldn't even have my usual after-work beer since Jewel moved in. "Not in front of the children." Not until last month, when I bought a little refrigerator and put it up in my room. That's where I kept my beer. I tried not to think an awful lot about the fact that that was *my* house.

But as I crested the hill I noticed something amiss. I noticed a man taking down the For Sale sign in front of the Munsky farm. The Munsky farm had been for sale now for about two years, ever since old Mrs. Munsky had been killed. Prophesy County wasn't what you'd call a bullish real estate market. The Munsky place and the place across the road that had been vacated not long after had both been on the market a long time. I glanced over there, at the former artist's residence. It was missing its For Sale sign, too.

Instead of pulling into my driveway, I went on down the hill to Falls End, a tourist camp at the bottom of the falls run by Haywood Hunter, who'd bought the place back after World War II on the GI Bill. Him and his wife, though I never knew her. She ran off with a salesman in an Airstream back in '54, leaving Haywood and their two boys to fend for themselves. The boys were long gone, but Haywood was there, as always. It being early fall and a weekday, Haywood didn't have any residents at the camp. He came out of his office to greet me as I pulled up, pulling on his big, bulbous nose, as is his custom.

"Hey, neighbor," he called, as I climbed out of the '55.

"Hey yourself. What's going on up at the Munsky place?"

"Got sold. Like that artist fella's place," he said, hiking up his khaki pants over his nonexistent ass. I always felt God had played a mean trick on old Haywood, giving him more in some places and leaving other places vacant. His huge honker, barrel chest, and bowed legs seemed hung together on nothing save a hand-tooled, Indian leather belt.

"Who to?"

"Where you been? Ain't been reading the papers, have ya?"

"What?"

"Course, it's all been on the back pages. I been meaning to talk to you about it, but I don't get out much any more."

"What, Haywood?"

"They made me an offer on my place, too. Good one."

"Who?"

"The Metropolis Developing Corporation out of Houston, Texas, that's who."

"What the hell's going on?"

He leaned against the wooden railing by the front porch of the office and grinned a mischievous grin. "You don't want yuppies as neighbors? That what you're trying to tell me?"

"Haywood, I'm in the middle of an investigation. I been interviewing people all day. I ain't had my dinner and all I got to look forward to is my sister's cooking. Stop messing with me."

"Okay. The Metropolis Developing Corporation of Houston, Texas, plans on turning Mountain Falls Road into a condo time-share project."

"What!"

"Condo time-share. It's—"

"I know what it is! Who in their right mind would wanna spend that much money up here?"

Haywood got defensive. "Well, it's a real pretty view, Milton."

"Right. Condo time-share. Jesus! How much they offering you?"

"I ain't at liberty to divulge that information."

"Shit."

I got in my car and drove back up the hill to my house. Jewel greeted me at the door. "You got a letter."

"I get lots of letters. Most of 'em bills. You know, to pay for the electricity for hair blowers, and water for forty-five showers a day, and gas so you can make cornmeal surprise—"

She threw the letter at me and walked off. I supposed I deserved it. I opened the letter while standing in the foyer. It was from the law firm of Klepper, Potter, Burns, and Task out of Oklahoma City. They wanted to meet with me to discuss my property. Why did I feel they just might represent the Metropolis Developing Corporation of Houston, Texas? Because I'm not totally stupid, that's why. I moved into the living room and picked up the phone and dialed Oklahoma City. But instead of calling the offices of Klepper, Potter, Burns and Task, I got the office of Billy Moulini.

Billy Moulini owns the property between me and the artist. It's a mountain cabin chateau built back in the fifties as a honeymoon lodge for Billy and his first wife. He and wife number four used it just last year. Wife number four's name was Wanda and she was nineteen at the time of the wedding. Billy was sixty-four. He made it big in plumbing.

After his secretary got him on the line, I asked, "Mr. Moulini, you heard anything about Metropolis Developing Corporation out of Houston, Texas?"

"Yeah. New outfit. Buying up half of Oklahoma. Time-share condos, I think. Why?"

"Because they just bought up the Munsky place and the place next to you and made Haywood Hunter an offer he's not likely to refuse."

"Well, fuck."

"Yes, sir."

"Double fuck."

"Yes, sir. And I just got me a letter from some law office in Oklahoma City wanting to discuss my property."

"You gonna sell?"

"Well, shit, Mr. Moulini! No way. I love this house. I don't wanna sell! You wanna sell?"

"Ain't no way. What's the name of the law outfit contacted you?"

"Klepper, Potter, Burns, and Task."

"Hum. I know Ralph Burns. Real asshole. Went in with him on a deal once almost bankrupted me. I figure if he's in on this deal, Mountain Falls Road could be in trouble."

"That's not good news."

"Not much is nowadays."

"Ain't that the truth."

"You wanna fight this, Milton?"

"Yes, sir. If we got a chance."

"You think Haywood would fight?"

"Well, I don't know. Gets kinda lonely down there at Falls End off-season."

"Talk to him. Meanwhile, I'll get my lawyer moving on injunctions and the like. See what we can do."

"Mr. Moulini, you think if we offered LeRoy Munsky the same deal he's getting from that outfit he'd sell to us instead?"

"Might be a way. I'll get back to you."

"Thank you, Mr. Moulini."

I didn't like Billy Moulini. He was loud, crass, slapped you on the back a lot, and smoked foul-smelling cigars. But I'd also never needed him before. I figured as an ally, he'd be better than a poke in the eye with a sharp stick. I wandered into the kitchen. Jewel was alone in there, slamming pots around. "Sorry about that earlier," I said.

She didn't turn around. She just kept slamming pots. "I said I was sorry."

She leaned against the sink and put her bad leg up on a footstool. "This isn't working," she said.

"Don't I know it."

That wasn't what I was supposed to say. I understood that immediately when she glared at me, shoved the footstool halfway across the kitchen, and slammed off to her bedroom just off the kitchen. Used to be my bedroom. Has a fireplace. Private bath. Real nice room. I followed her. "Jewel Anne. Calm down."

She whirled around, almost losing her balance because of the bad leg. By the by, there is absolutely nothing wrong with my sister's leg. The problem's in her brain. There's a little bitty old fragment of a bullet lodged somewhere up there in that part of her brain that tells her left leg what to do. For about eight months now, that part of her brain's been real quiet. Won't tell her leg a damn thing.

Screaming at me, she said, "Calm down? You drag me and my kids up here so we can all pretend to be one great big happy family and then you want to throw us out and you say calm down?"

"I'm not throwing you out!"

"Oh, really?"

"Sit down on the bed, okay?"

"Don't worry yourself about my health. I'm fine."

Strangling her entered my mind. I pushed it aside. "That letter I got was from some outfit buying up most of Mountain Falls Road. I think they're gonna make an offer on this place."

She stiffened. "You gonna take it?"

"Not if I can help it. I just talked to Billy Moulini—"

"That reprobate!"

"Well, yeah, but he's a rich and influential reprobate. And he doesn't want to sell either."

"What's going to happen, Milton? Is there a chance my kids and I are going to be living under a bridge?"

I laughed. I couldn't help it. "Jewel, you got over half a million dollars stashed away—"

"In CDs that would lose the interest if I took 'em out, in municipal bonds that don't mature for five more years, et cetera, et cetera, et cetera. As they say, Milton, my cash flow isn't liquid at the moment."

"We'll work it out," I said, the words as lame as my sister's leg.

"We may work out the problems with somebody trying to buy the house, but will we ever work out the problems you and I are having?"

I shrugged my shoulders and kept quiet.

"Are you going to talk to me or just stand there like the dummy Mama always claimed you were?"

"Jewel, you nag me more than LaDonna ever did!"

"I do not!"

"You do! You're always telling me what to do and how to do it! I can't even drink a beer in my own damned living room—"

"Watch your—"

"Language? Watch my language! That's what I'm talking about!"

"Well, you cuss like a sailor, Milton, I swear you do!"

"That's my right! This is my house! I can cuss in my own house if I want to! I can drink beer in my house if I want to! I can leave my shorts in the god-damn living room if I want to!"

Jewel stood up and walked quietly to the closet, opened the door, and pulled out a suitcase. "I'll send for the rest later. Please tell each of my children to pack a small bag."

"Jewel Anne!" I grabbed her arm and led her as gently as my temper allowed to the bed and sat her down. "You wanted to know how I felt! That's how I feel. Okay? Those are my feelings. Now I want to hear your feelings."

Silence. "Come on. Tell me how you feel about this whole situation."

"You're a slob. You're dirty. All you do is cuss and swill beer! Carl's growing allergic to your cat who sheds all over my furniture and sprays the walls! If I could get up those stairs, I'd be afraid to look in your room! Marlene has to clean up after you in the bathroom. You forgot to lift the lid one night! That's disgusting! And you always forget to put the lid down!"

"Do my bathroom habits have to come into this?"

"Do you want my feelings or not?"

"Okay, okay."

"You spend the night out with that woman of yours and the kids know exactly what you're doing!"

"Rather than keep it quiet like their daddy did?"

"Milton! That's not fair!"

"Right."

"You get phone calls in the middle of the night because your deputies are too stupid to handle anything themselves...."

"If I can't mention your late husband, you can't mention my deputies!"

"Deal. You've never offered to even clean off the table! You don't turn your clothes right side out when you put them in the laundry! You get ice out of the freezer and never fill up the icetray! I've caught you drinking straight out of the milk bottle! And you put wet towels in the hamper and mildew everything in there—"

"I did that once."

"And you—"

"Are you anywhere near through?"

"And you drive me insane."

"You never offered once to even buy groceries," I said. "I pay for everything. House note, utilities, food."

"I do all the cooking and cleaning."

"I'm paying for your kids' food as well as yours!"

"Marlene cleans your bathroom 'cause I can't get up stairs!"

"You ever seen Marlene's idea of a clean bathroom?"

She jumped up and headed for the suitcase. "Jewel Anne, sit your ass down before I swat it!"

"You promised the kids horses."

"I'm supposed to pay for that, too?"

"I'm supposed to clean that up, too?"

We sat and glared at each other. I think possibly there's a problem with adults living in the same house and not having sex. How long do most roommates of the same sex, heterosexual roommates, last? How long could Jewel Anne and I possibly last? I didn't feel up to committing the ultimate sin to make things work better.

"We need help," Jewel finally said, her voice actually quiet and somewhat calm.

"What kinda help?"

"Remember that counselor the kids and I went to for grief therapy when we first got here?"

"I'm not going to any goddamn shrink!"

I got up and out and went up the stairs to my room and my beer. I popped a top and guzzled half of the can, then sat down with my notebook and started going over the Bell case as a way of not thinking of my domestic problems. But I kept coming back to the same things. How come an army corporal had a pair of captain's bars and a marine tattoo up his ass? And where did that knot on Lois Bell's head come from? And when? Did she fall down in the bathtub and get so depressed about it she decided to end it all? Or did husband Bill knock her around so much she decided to end it all? Except Dr. Jim didn't say anything about bruises and contusions, which would be there if she'd been an abused wife. No, all she had was a crack on the head. But when did she get it and where did it come from? Since I didn't know the answers to those questions, I decided to write down what I did know. I opened my little book I keep and wrote: "1) Get another look at cpt.'s bars, 2) send Mr.'s fingerprints to FBI." Then I went down to suffer supper with my family.

WHEN THE GUARD UNLOCKED the bank's doors the next morning, I was there. The court order got me back in and I headed straight to the captain's bars. They were pinned through a small piece of cardboard with the stud on the other side. I loosened them and looked at the backs. Remembering my favorite officer in the air force had clued me in to look there. He was a lieutenant, and on the back of his bars, he'd had engraved "Fuck the AF." On the back of the bars in my hand were the same initials as on the wedding rings, and a date—I suppose the date of the commission—January 14, 1973. So the captain's bars more than likely didn't belong to anybody's grandpa. I went back to the station and called Dr. Jim at his office at the hospital.

"Hey, Dr. Jim, it's Milt."

"Milton."

"Do me a favor."

"Depends."

"Pull me some fingerprints on William Bell, Sr."

"Okay. You got anybody claiming these bodies? Technically, I can keep 'em here forever in my freezer, but I'd just as soon not."

"I'm working on it," I said and hung up, thinking about Doctor Jim's new freezer. Last year I'd been really P.O.'d when he got it, knowing the only way he did was 'cause his brother-in-law was on the County Commission. Because of that, Dr. Jim had stuff some of the big city morgues didn't have. Like that walk-in freezer that would hold up to ten bodies. While the Sheriff's Department had three of five units in the shop two weeks out of every month. But now, what with the Bell family and all, I wasn't so begrudging of Dr. Jim's freezer. I had longer than I normally would. Shit, according to an article I read in the paper recently, I had forever. Houston had a body on ice that had been there for ten years. Why, I don't even want to think about.

I called the Longbranch elementary school where the two older kids had gone to school, and made an appointment to meet with the principal and the kids' teachers for that afternoon. Then I called the law offices of Klepper, Potter, Burns, and Task collect, identified myself, and asked for the person who'd signed the letter I'd received, namely Arnold Task.

"Task."

"Mr. Task, this is Milton Kovak from Prophesy County. I have a house on Mountain Falls Road."

"Of course, Mr. Kovak! So glad you called! I take it you got my letter! That's great! Hope maybe you and I can meet, at your convenience, of course, to discuss a matter of mutual benefit! You interested? Of course you are!"

"Mr. Task—"

"As you may know, there is a lot of interest these days in that whole Mountain Falls area! And, Mr. Kovak, you're in the catbird seat on this one! I mean to tell ya! Let's have lunch sometime soon!"

"Mr. Task—"

"Friday? Is Friday good for you? Of course, I'll come to Longbranch and meet you! I hear the Longbranch Inn has a great lunch buffet! How 'bout we meet at the Longbranch Inn, say noonish Friday? Sound good, Mr. Kovak? My treat, naturally, ha, ha!"

"Mr. Task—"

"It was great talking with you, Mr. Kovak! I'll see you Friday at noon! Bye!"

The line went dead in my hand. I have never taken kindly to being sandbagged. I got the feeling that was what had just happened. I redialed the Oklahoma City number collect and told the receptionist to take a message for Mr. Task. "Tell him," I said, "that I won't be able to make it Friday. Or Monday, or Tuesday, or Wednesday, or Thursday. Tell him I don't need a free lunch. Tell him I'm not selling my property. For any price. Got that?"

"Sir, would you like to speak to Mr. Task?"

"Not in a million years!" I hung up.

FOUR

"THEY WERE SUCH a nice, quiet family! The children were always well behaved in class and on the playground. I only saw the parents the once, when they both came in to register the kids at the first of the year. Quiet, nice people. It just seems so unbelievable that this could have happened!"

"Yes, ma'am," I said. Mrs. Oshley was the principal of the Davis Road Elementary School where the two older Bell children had attended classes. She was relatively new to Longbranch herself, having come here with her husband less than ten years earlier. Takes awhile in a small town to lose the new-person image. Like about four generations.

"You have the papers here where they registered the kids?"

"Sure do. What do you need to know?"

"Next of kin other than the mom and dad, last school, that sorta thing."

Mrs. Oshley studied her papers for a moment, then shook her head. "No next of kin, except the parents, of course. And, I remember now, when Mrs. Bell signed the children up, she said there'd been a fire at the last school the children had attended and it would be awhile before they could get the paperwork to us. That was last year, in the middle of the school year when the children transferred.'' She shook her head again. ''Somehow we forgot to ask her about it this year. These things can slip past us, you know.''

''Yes, ma'am,'' I said, ''I know how that goes.''

We heard the door open behind us.

''Here's Mrs. Munroe now,'' the principal said, standing. I did likewise. Mrs. Oshley was about forty, short and on the pudgy side, with brown hair losing the battle to gray. Mrs. Munroe was the exact opposite. At least my height and she didn't look old enough to have graduated high school, much less college. I figured there had to be an Indian in her background someplace when I saw her coal-black hair hanging down to her waist, her black eyes, and olive complexion. And there wasn't an extra ounce of flesh on her anywhere. An attractive lady if you were into anorexia, which I never have been. Mrs. Oshley introduced us and we shook hands.

''Billy was in my class,'' she said.

''I was hoping you could tell me a little something about the family. Mainly I'm looking for next of kin. Like a grandma, something like that. Billy ever mention anything like that?''

Mrs. Munroe shook her head. ''He was a very quiet child. Never called attention to himself. Always polite, though, and always answered when called on. Gosh, Mr. Kovak, I can't think of anything that could help you! Maybe one of the children?" She looked at the principal as if for guidance. "But to tell you the truth, I can't even think of any particular child he was close to. On the playground, he always played in a group. Fairly good in sports, nothing spectacular though. Just an average kid."

The door to the principal's office opened again and we were joined by a second teacher, this one the infamous Mr. Crouch. Infamous because he was the only male teacher below the high school level in the whole county. Naturally, that made him strange.

His answer to the same question about the daughter, Melissa, was basically the same. All he could add was, "Sometimes she'd start crying for no apparent reason, but that happens with first graders. Away from home for the first time, that sort of thing. I met the mother at an open house. Of course, I already knew her from the bank. A nice lady." He shook his tightly curled dark head. "It's just unbelievable."

That was the consensus all right. Unbelievable. This kind of thing just didn't happen.

"The only thing I can suggest, Deputy, if the teachers agree," Mrs. Oshley said, "is that maybe you could speak to each class. Maybe one of the children could offer something we can't."

"That's not a bad idea," Mrs. Munroe said. "I think it might help them to deal with this whole thing a little better if they could be involved in some way.

And, Officer, some of the children have been asking about the funeral?''

I shook my head. "I wish I could tell you, ma'am. Unless we find the next of kin . . . well . . .''

"If you don't find the next of kin, what will happen?'' Mr. Crouch asked.

I cleared my throat. "Cremation.''

All three educators looked at each other, then the women looked down at their feet. Mr. Crouch just glared at me. I felt a little guilty.

"Well, let's go talk to the kids,'' Mr. Crouch suggested.

Kids never cease to amaze me. The first graders wanted to know if Melissa was in heaven and whether or not she liked it there. I assured them she was probably having a hell of a time. The third graders wanted to know where their parents could send flowers, and asked me what kinds seemed appropriate. I fielded that one through Mrs. Munroe.

But nobody, not one kid, could tell me anything I didn't already know. After leaving the children, I went back to Mrs. Oshley's office to thank her for her help.

"I wish I could have done more.'' She walked down the hall with me to the door of the school. Once there, she stopped and looked hesitant.

"Mr. Kovak?''

"Yes, ma'am?''

"Could you keep me informed about the next of kin? I mean, if you find them? Or if you don't. I don't want those children . . . well . . ."

"Yes, ma'am. I'll let you know before the county does anything."

"Thank you, Mr. Kovak."

I got in the squad car and headed for the station, new thoughts entering my head. Look, I watch television. I read books. I know the ways of the world. I wasn't born yesterday. I started adding up the things I now knew, that there were no records of anything older than 1986, nowhere had I found any birthday cards or Christmas cards or letters from anybody outside Longbranch, the marine tattoo and the captain's bars belonging to somebody supposedly a corporal in the army, the fact that the oldest son, Billy, had no close friends at all, and the overall fact that nobody knew anything about the Bell family told me one thing: These people were hiding. There were only two scenarios that sprang to mind: The Bells were wanted and on the lam, or this had something to do with the Witness Protection Program. The fingerprints on Bill Bell I was getting from Dr. Jim should tell the tale.

I decided another look at the Bell house was in order and swung by there before heading to the station. I still had the key in my pocket, so I had no problem going in. The place was as filthy as it had been, just no dead bodies in it. I stood in the living

room looking around, finding nothing to jump out
at me and say "See, here I am. The answer to your
questions." I didn't feel up to the kitchen or the
bathroom, and I couldn't see anything much being
in the kids' room, so I ended up in the master bedroom again.

Unlike the children's bed, Lois and Bill's bed
wasn't just a mattress on the floor but an actual bed
on a frame. I decided to look under it. Along with a
hell of a lot of dust bunnies, I found a stash of magazines. I began pulling them out, half expecting
Penthouse or *Hustler,* but found instead lots and lots
of back issues of *Machine Design, Engineering Digest,* and *NASA Tech Briefs.* I sat down on the floor
and looked at them. Engineering magazines. In the
home of a garage mechanic and a bank teller? So Bill
was a garage mechanic by day and by hobby an engineer? Hardly likely. But it did fit in with my theory that Lois and Bill Bell had had previous lives
elsewhere.

I picked up one issue of *Engineering Digest* and
began leafing idly through the pages. Something on
page twenty grabbed my attention. There was a picture of a man in a suit with a caption under the picture that said "Grady Grimes promoted to Vice
President of Engineering, Warrick Corporation, after his successful patent of the SCR Coolant System." But that, of course, wasn't what caught my
attention. The red-inked scrawl across the man's face

was what had stopped me at that page. It read "Fuck up!!!" Not knowing exactly why, I rolled up the magazine, and stuck it in my back pocket and left the filth behind me, heading for the office.

Back in my office, I decided it was time to contact Oklahoma City. I called the hospital first, the one where the youngest child had been born. But they wouldn't tell me anything unless my request was in writing. So much for that. The address on the W2 forms I found in the safe deposit box told me little. Just a number and a street in a city filled with numbers and streets. I called the Oklahoma City Police Department and got put through to their liaison officer, whatever the hell that meant. His name was Leon Purdue.

"Yes, sir, Deputy? What can I do for you?"

I explained my situation.

"Awful. Plumb awful. But how can I help?"

"I got a W2 here for 1986 shows they lived in your city at that time." I gave him the street and number. "I know they didn't own the house. They rented here, probably rented there. Maybe you could get me to the landlord, something like that?"

"Why don't you give me your number and I'll see what I can come up with? May take awhile though. We're pretty understaffed around here."

"Ain't we all."

"You said it."

I gave him the number and rang off, thinking about where I was going with this investigation. Namely nowhere. If I didn't turn up something in a big hurry, the Bell family would end up a little pile of ashes. I liked that thought about as much as the school teachers had.

I sat in my office and stared at the county road map tacked to my wall. The door opened and Mike Neils, one of the day deputies, stuck his head in. "Messenger just came by with them fingerprints you asked Dr. Jim for."

I straightened up. "Great. Send 'em off to D.C. for me, will ya? Federal Express. Overnight. We still got that account with them?"

"I think so. I'll check with Gladys."

I resumed my map staring. At five-thirty, I realized I'd stared at that map with very little result for a very long time. Of course, the alternative to map staring was going home. And going home meant facing Jewel. As bad as I already felt, I'd as soon have stripped naked in the K-mart as go home to my sister. I picked up the phone and dialed the number for the Longbranch Inn and asked for Glenda Sue Robinson. After a long minute, she came on the line.

"Hi," I said. "Whaja doing?"

"Hi. Working. What're you doing?"

"Nothing. What time you get off?"

"It's Thursday."

"I know it's Thursday. You ever hear of spontaneity?"

"Vaguely. But never to do with you."

"Very funny. What time do you get off?"

"Working till ten tonight."

"Shit."

"What's up?"

"I don't wanna go home."

"I've heard that one before, but usually from married men."

"What married men?"

"It was a joke."

"Not very goddamn funny."

"God, you're in a lovely mood."

"Can't you trade shifts with somebody?"

"If I'm willing to give up my Friday night."

I was silent for a minute. I heard Glenda Sue say, "Milton? You still there?"

"Yeah, I'm here."

"Go home. I'll see you tomorrow."

"I don't wanna go home." I tried not to notice the whine in my voice. And hoped she didn't either.

"Jesus, you sound like my daughter when she was ten years old!" Okay, so she noticed. "Go home. Be good." She hung up. I hung up. And stared at the map some more. Finally, after another ten minutes of geography, I got up and headed for my '55 in the parking lot.

It was almost seven when I pulled into the driveway. I noticed Jewel's car was gone. Inside the house, stuck to the refrigerator with a little smiley-faced magnet, was a note: "Open house at the Jr. Hi! Your supper's in the oven. Be back around ten. J." I sighed a sigh of relief and opened the oven door.

The piece of meat on the plate had a gray tinge to it and the potatoes were raw. I persuaded the slop down the garbage disposal, opened a can of tuna fish, and went up to my room for a beer, which I brought down to the living room. I turned on the television to a *Perry Mason* rerun and sat down with my tuna and my beer, propped my feet up on the coffee table and had a grand old time. Evinrude, my orange tabby cat, discovered that sitting in my lap and eating half my tuna was a fun thing for him to do. On my second trip upstairs for beer, I just decided to bring down the whole six pack.

For some reason, it reminded me of a time when I was a kid, maybe seven or eight, years before Jewel Anne was born, when Daddy had to go on an overnight trip for some reason. Mama made a picnic and we ate it at the coffee table in front of the TV watching *Sky King*. It was one of those things that stick in your mind when you're brought up never watching TV while you eat and always eating at the kitchen table "like a family oughta." I don't know if Mama ever mentioned it to Daddy, but to me it was our secret. A special night nobody knew about but her and me. After my long six months of my sister's cooking and my sister's rules, this was definitely one of those special nights. Just me and Evinrude.

By ten o'clock the evidence of my evening of debauchery was destroyed. No remnants remained except the cat's occasional burp. By five after ten I was drumming my fingers on the arm of my chair in anticipation of the arrival of the troops. By ten-thirty I was on the horn to the school to see if the open house had gone on longer than anticipated. There was no answer. By ten forty-five, I was in my '55 heading toward Longbranch on Highway 5, trying to take the same route Jewel would have to get to the junior high.

I saw the white station wagon pulled over to the side of the road on a long deserted stretch about ten miles from town and eight miles from home. The hood was up and the car was facing me so I couldn't tell if anyone was in it. I passed and made a U-turn on the highway, pulling up behind the wagon. Inside I could see heads turning toward me. For the first time in almost an hour, I unclenched my fists.

As I bailed out of my car, I saw the doors fly open on the station wagon and my family come rushing toward me, all talking at once.

"Boy, Uncle Milt—"

"Milton, it just stopped—"

"Why didn't you find a phone—"

"I was so scared—"

"Dumbest thing—"

"Well, I figured you'd figure—"

"As long as everybody's okay—"

"Just get me home, I gotta pee—"

We locked up the station wagon and all piled into the '55 and headed back to Mountain Falls Road and home.

On Friday morning, as I walked into the station house half an hour late from having to take care of Jewel's car, Gladys greeted me with "Well, we had another one."

"Suicide?" I'd been thinking about the Bells.

She looked at me like I'd just peed in her oatmeal. "No. Peaches."

"How many and where?"

"Four cases at the Chat and Chew."

"What's Bernie doing with four cases of peaches in the first place?"

"Well, his wife's name's Melba." She didn't crack a smile.

"Gladys, that was a joke!"

"Actually, it was supposed to be for their new diet special. I was really looking forward to it, too. Hamburger patty, cottage cheese, and peaches?"

"Yum, yum," I said in that sarcastic way that women the world over have learned to hate.

She turned and walked away. I've known Gladys five years. That's the second time I've heard her make a joke, so, obviously, she's not totally humorless, she just seems that way. But my sarcasm should teach her a lesson.

I went down the hall to the sheriff's office. "Morning," I greeted from his open door.

"Morning. Peaches."

"I heard."

"How many's that make?"

"Six burglaries in three years. Total of about a hundred cases of peaches."

"Think we got us a loony running around?"

"I think we got us a bunch of loonies running around, but I don't know if any of 'em like peaches."

"Well, get Dalton on it."

"Yes, sir."

Dalton had become our resident peach robbery expert. Each burglary had been given to him. Sometimes, to myself alone, I figured if we gave the case (no pun intended) to somebody else, maybe we'd get out of the pits (really, no pun intended). I walked into the deputy bullpen, told Dalton it was his, and went back to my office to worry about my own problems, mainly the Bells. I knew it'd take a good two weeks to get anything back on those fingerprints, it always did. What to do, what to do. I turned around a couple of times in my swivel chair, stared out the window some, stared at the map some, then called Glenda Sue.

"We on tonight?" I asked.

"Is it Friday?"

"Yeah."

"Then, unless you're trying to tell me something, we're on."

"What would I be trying to tell you?"

"That you'd rather spend time at home with your sister?"

"Funny as a dead armadillo."

"What do you wanna do?"

"When?"

"Tonight!"

"Usual."

"Milton, you got no imagination."

"What do you wanna do?"

"I dunno."

"Well, you brought it up."

"Bowling?"

"I hate bowling."

"There's a dance at the VFW hall."

"I don't dance, you know that."

"So it's Mexican food and my place."

"If you don't wanna..." I didn't like the way the conversation was going. Why did she want to change a good thing? Why do women always want more, more, more!

"No. That's fine."

"Doesn't sound fine."

"Really. It's fine." The "really" sounded about as soft as a ten-penny nail.

"If you wanna go to the VFW tonight, that's fine," I said.

"No. Forget it."

"No. I'm serious. It's fine!"

"Oh, we'd just have loads of fun watching everybody else dance."

"I'll dance, I'll dance."

"Forget it."

"Jesus, Glenda Sue!"

"I'll see you when I see you," she said, as she hung up. I wasn't doing too well with women that week, and that's the God's truth.

FIVE

"YOU MISSED THE TURNOFF," Glenda Sue said from the passenger side of the car. Way over at the far end of the passenger side of the car. About as far over as you could get and still be in the car. The nice thing about driving a '55 is having your lady sitting there next to you, able to help you shift while you were busy copping a feel.

"I didn't miss nothing," I said.

"Aren't we going to Maria's?"

"No."

"Then where are we going? If you pull up in front of the VFW hall, I swear to God I'm not getting out of the car." She crossed her arms over her still-nice bosom and glared out the windshield.

"I'm not going to the VFW hall."

"Then where are we going?"

"To the drive-in."

"I'm not really in the mood for greasy hamburgers, thank you very much."

"Not that kind of drive-in."

"The drive-in movies? The Twin closed down four years ago, Milt! Where were you?"

"Just hush up for a minute, okay?"

"I'll hush up for life!"

Ahead of us on the highway was the ghost of passion, the distant memory of desire, the echo of hormones gone mad, the defunct drive-in theater. The marquee sign's glass was shattered, and the single letter S hung cock-eyed, the last brave remnant of a dying art form.

Part of the trim on the sign had fallen off, leaving gaping holes where mud daubers built their miniature cities. Johnson grass took hold of the asphalt drive leading to the ticket booth, leaving no doubt that man no longer belonged in this world that resembled Hollywood's idea of the day after. The glass of the ticket booth, which had shielded teenage attendants from the elements for four generations, was shattered, its fragments scattered inside and out.

I pulled in and slowly drove past the booth up to the chain and padlock that kept the riffraff out of the acreage beyond. One of the good things about being with the sheriff's department is that you get keys to just about any locked object in the county. I got out of the car, used the key I'd borrowed to unlock the padlock, and pulled the chain off the driveway.

"What in the hell do you think you're doing?" Glenda Sue asked.

"Hush, now," I said, grinning slyly.

I pulled the '55 into the theater complex and up close to the screen where there was a wide flat area with some rotting playground equipment on it. I stood for a minute looking at the jungle gym and teeter-totter, remembering me and Bobby Abrams pushing Tommy Anderson off the slide and almost breaking his leg. Aw, the good old days.

I shut off the engine and got out, taking my keys to the trunk. Glenda Sue sat in the car pretending not to watch while I pulled out my booty and set it up. An old card table and two folding chairs; Jewel Anne's second best tablecloth I'd snuck out of the house; Leonard's jam box he'd loaned me for the occasion; and two brand-new Willie Nelson tapes. Then I brought out the box with the take-out Mexican food, the bottle of champagne, and the Coleman lantern. Yeah, candles would have been sexier, but they'd have blown out. There's something to be said for practicality.

I set everything up on the table, placing the plastic utensils just so, stuck a tape in the recorder and turned it on, and lit the lantern. Then I walked over to the car and gallantly, with as Errol Flynn a flourish as I could muster, opened the car door.

"Would madam like to take her seat now?" I asked, bowing from the waist.

"I swear, Milt, you slay me." But she grinned and got out of the car. That evening was a milestone of sorts. It was the first time I'd made it all the way with a girl in a drive-in. Childhood fantasy realized. It wasn't bad at all, even if my back did holler a little about the cramped quarters.

I got her back to her trailer house around one in the morning, and the kissing we did at the door was the sweetest in a long time.

"You're full of surprises, Deputy," Glenda Sue said in a half whisper.

"Like to keep my lady guessing," I whispered back.

She giggled, kissed me again, and went inside and I drove on to my house. Feeling pretty righteous. It doesn't take a hell of a lot to make a woman happy, I finally figured. Just a little attention, something out of the ordinary every now and then, and a willingness to listen. I figured Glenda Sue was just damned lucky to have me. That's what I finally figured.

SATURDAY JEWEL ANNE AND I walked around the stable and horse pen area. Looking at it. Trying to figure out how much money it would take to get the place in shape again to house horses.

"How much does a horse cost?" she asked.

"Couple of hundred, I suppose."

"I don't suppose we could get away with just one horse?"

"What do you think?"

"Three horses."

"You don't want one?"

She laughed. It had been awhile since I'd heard it. It reminded me of Mama's laugh. Jewel was a lot like

Mama in a lot of ways. Just took a long time for me to figure that out.

"Can you see me on a horse?"

"Why not?"

"This leg for one."

"You ride a horse with your butt, not your leg."

She shook her head. "I think I'll pass."

"Jewel—"

She turned to face me. "What?"

"How we gonna pay for the horses?"

She sighed. "You really are uptight about money, aren't you?"

"Yeah, well, I don't have a half-a-million nest egg to fall back on, lady."

"I'll buy the horses."

"I thought maybe we'd split the cost."

"I'll buy the horses."

"Jewel—"

"Milton, I'll buy the damned horses."

"No, we'll split the cost, okay? I'm just wondering if maybe we'd best hold off until we find out about this time-share condo business."

"I thought you weren't selling?"

"Not outright. But you know how these people are. They come into an area, you either sell or—"

Jewel laughed and turned around and headed for the house. "They'll burn us to the ground, right? Put poison in the well? Milt, you and your conspiracies!"

"What? What'd I say? I'm not talking about conspiracies—" But nobody was listening. I swear to God, you mention one little conspiracy and people act like that's all you ever talk about.

Sunday, we drove into Longbranch to the First Baptist Church. I'd gone some right after my wife and I split up, but when I moved up to Mountain Falls Road, I slid back to my old habits. Now that Jewel was here, though, backsliding was something she didn't tolerate. Like swearing and beer drinking. We all had Sunday dinner at the Longbranch Inn, one of the few meals a week I looked forward to.

Of all the things about my ex-wife, the bad and the good, the one that I really missed was her cooking. Then I thought about Dwayne Dickey getting all those good meals and almost missed my mouth with my fork. I thought about her buttermilk pancakes with the fresh sausage she used to buy from the pig farmer outside of town, her fresh-squeezed orange juice, and the dark roast coffee she used to make. Then I thought about Dwayne Dickey coming to the breakfast table in his bathrobe, maybe patting LaDonna on the rump as he passed her at the stove. Then I thought maybe I'd arrest him for something.

I drove Jewel and the kids back home and left them there and went over to Glenda Sue's. We hadn't made a date but Sunday was usually an okay day. But when I pulled up to her trailer house, her car was gone. I sat in mine for a while, feeling the warm autumn sun shining on me through the open car window and thinking dark thoughts. Thinking maybe Dwayne Dickey or somebody like him might be with Glenda Sue at this very minute. Why not? Dwayne had my wife, why not my girlfriend, too? Finally I started the car up and drove to the station.

As I didn't feel like map staring on a Sunday, I stared out the window instead. I needed something. Somebody to tell me what the hell happened to the Bells would be nice. Or maybe just a lead on a next of kin. But I was beginning to believe that there was no such animal. Lois and Bill Bell seemed made of whole cloth, never to have existed before 1986. The three children could have just as easily been Cabbage Patch dolls for all the good their birth certificate did me. After an hour of absolutely nothing, I left the station.

I headed in the opposite direction of home and, in twenty minutes, ended up at Rufus Dudley's horse farm, or as I used to call him when I was a kid, Uncle Rufe. He wasn't really an uncle, just a guy my daddy worked with on the oil rigs for twenty years or more. But he'd been a fixture at our house before Jewel was born. When the baby was no more than a few weeks old, Uncle Rufe met Vivian. A henna-haired divorcée with three kids and lots of bills, according to Mama's rendition of it all, which I listened to late at night while I was supposed to be asleep. They'd talk, Mama and Daddy, about Uncle

Rufe and Vivian for hours, Daddy saying Rufe needed a woman in his life, and Mama saying maybe so, but that woman wasn't Vivian Ellis. When Rufe up and married her (with Mama saying number four must be on its way), the friendship, which was being strained anyway, sorta tore apart.

I don't think there ever was a big fight or anything, just that Mama and Vivian didn't get along and the two couples gradually stopped seeing each other. The last time I'd seen Uncle Rufe had been at Mama's funeral, a shadowy little man with bowed legs, standing at the back of the sanctuary, his best felt cowboy hat held between his hands. And finally, after all those years, it finally dawned on me what all the fuss had been about. Rufe had had a thing about my mama. Instead of making me mad, when it dawned on me, it just made me all the sadder. I suppose Mama must have known, though knowing Mama I know she didn't do anything about it. But she must have been happy in those days, with her two men showing her attention and affection. And Vivian had been nothing but an interloper, taking away one of her menfolk.

By the time Mama died, Vivian had been buried for over ten years, and the three kids (there never had been a number four) were long gone God only knows where. Why Rufe and Mama, with Daddy gone before even Vivian, had never gotten together, I suppose only they knew. But that day at Mama's funeral, after we got to the cemetery, I went and got Uncle Rufe and had him come sit with the family. Because, if the truth be known, he'd been more family than any of the aunts and cousins lining the front seats, imports from as far away as Little Rock and Natchez.

To my shame, I hadn't seen Uncle Rufe since that day, almost five years before. And this day was only the second time I'd ever driven to the horse ranch he and Vivian had bought with his retirement from the refinery, a bank loan, and a lot of prayers. Sometimes you think, when you live in the same place with somebody, that there will always be time. Always be time to run into 'em on the street, or drive by and say hidy. And then there never is.

I pulled up the long drive between rows of white-washed fencing to the modest frame house Uncle Rufe lived in. The stables were five times bigger than the house, and a hundred times fancier. But that was business, not just living. I honked my horn and slid out of the car. From the opened door of the entrance to the stable area, I saw Uncle Rufe. He was shorter and more bowlegged than he'd been five years before. As he drew closer, though, I noticed that not much about him had changed. His skin was so weathered it looked like good saddle leather, creased with years and use.

When he finally recognized me, the leathery face broke into a grin, showing dentures white as snow, even as a picket fence, and as natural looking as plastic flowers in a graveyard.

"Well, I'll be goddamned! Milty, you rascal, what you doing here?"

"Hey there, Uncle Rufe." We shook hands and then stood surveying his land. "Nice-looking place."

"Thank you, thank you." We stood for a while longer, looking over the acres of prancing horse-flesh. "What brings you out this way?" he finally asked.

"Horses," I said, grinning.

"Well, I got a few."

"Yes, sir, you surely do."

"You in a buying mood?"

"No, sir, I'm in a talking-about-buying mood."

"Nearly the same," he said, spitting a wad of tobacco juice two feet toward the fence. "If I remember rightly, though, boy, you never did have you a good seat."

"That's the truth. Damned things scare me half to death, ever since that old Jesse of yours bit me on the ass."

He roared with laughter, almost choking on his chaw of tobacco. "That weren't no bite, boy, just a friendly little nip to get you moving."

I shook my head and laughed with him. "All the same, Uncle Rufe...."

"So, why you here then?"

"You know Jewel Anne and her kids moved in with me?"

He nodded his head. "Heard about that. My condolences on the loss of her husband."

"Thank you. Anyhow, I got me a stable and corral on my property, and the kids are interested in getting some horses so the place won't look so empty. I thought I'd just sorta figure out how much this would cost me."

"How many horses you figuring on?"

"Just three. One for each kid. Otherwise, they'd end up playing tug-a-war and—"

"Get theirselves nipped in the ass?" We laughed some more before we got down to business. "Come on," he said, and led me into the stable area.

There must have been about fifty horses galloping around the fields, and inside the stable there were at least ten more, standing in their stalls. He went up to a light-brown one with a glint in its eye I didn't much care for. I kept imagining it looking around me for my ass and licking its chops.

Rubbing the head of the horse, he said, "This chestnut here's a fifteen-year-old mare, just a yard horse with a hay belly, but gentle as Mother Teresa. Can let you have her for seven hundred."

"Seven hundred? For one horse?"

He looked hurt. "Boy, that's two hundred less than I'd let her go to anybody else."

I looked at the horse eyeing me and sizing me up. "Uncle Rufe, I know you're not trying to cheat me. That's not what I'm saying at all. It's just that I had no idea it would cost this much."

He leaned against the gate of the mare's stall and pulled off another plug of tobacco and stuck it in his jaw. "Boy," he said, spitting immediately, "you wanna talk about cost, we'll talk about cost. 'Cause the buying of the flesh itself is just the beginning. You know anything about feed, tack, and all that shit?"

"No, sir."

"We're talking a minimum of two hundred a month in maintenance on three horses."

"You're shitting me."

"I wouldn't shit you, boy, you're my favorite turd."

"Uncle Rufe, I'm gonna have to think on this awhile."

"Well, boy, while you're doing that, come on in the house and let me buy you a beer. How's that sound?"

Rubbing sweat off my forehead, I said, "Sounds better than a poke in the eye with a sharp stick."

"Don't it though?"

We went in the house, me marveling at the cleanliness. An old man alone and the house was as clean as Jewel's. "Got me an Indian woman comes in twice a week. Alls I gotta do is pick up my underwear. She does the rest.''

In the kitchen he opened two bottles of beer and we leaned against the counter, drinking and talking about my mama and daddy. In about an hour I left, heading back home to Mountain Falls Road.

It was close on suppertime when I pulled in the driveway, and I wondered about the little Japanese car I didn't recognize sitting in the driveway. I got out of my '55 and headed in the house. Jewel Anne greeted me from the living room.

"Milton, come on in here," she said, smiling, which in itself was unusual. "There's someone here I want you to meet."

I went in, smiling a greeting at the lady sitting on the sofa. She stood and extended her hand, which I shook. She was about five foot nothing, with short brown hair and wearing a suit. She had freckles on the bridge of her nose and looked for all the world like a little girl playing dress-up in her mama's best power outfit.

"Milton, this is Margaret Marston. She'll be staying for dinner."

"Glad to meet you, Miss Marston," I said.

"Why don't you go get washed up and we'll be eating in a minute," Jewel said.

I left the room and headed upstairs, wondering who our guest was and where I'd heard the name Marston before. It was while I was soaping my hands that it dawned on me. Marston. As in Dr. Marston. The shrink my sister and the kids had gone to for grief therapy after moving up here. Well, I'll be goddamned. The sneaky little brat! Jewel'd obviously brought the woman in to observe me, see what she, poor Jewel, had to put up with. But I planned to turn the tables on my daddy's little darling.

Jewel had set the table in the dining room, rather than use the breakfast room as was usual. Going to the table, I held out the good doctor's chair and then sat down next to her. After a little light dinner talk, Jewel's way of distracting the lady from the mess she'd served, I said, "Marston. Marston. Aren't you Dr. Marston, the psychologist?"

She smiled. "Yes, that's right."

"You know, I was thinking of coming to see you." I suppressed a giggle as Jewel choked on her food. "I got this real interesting case I could use your input on."

"Oh, really?"

"Yes, ma'am. I'm chief deputy at the sheriff's department, ya know?" She nodded. Of course she knew. She probably knew what I'd eaten for breakfast that morning and on which side I tucked my jewels. "Well, you may have heard about the suicide-accident we had here recently?" Again she nodded her head. "Well, there's some interesting things about it. The lady of the house worked at the bank, very neat in her dress and hair and all that, and the kids were always clean at school, but..." And then I went into a detailed account of all the filth in the house, embellishing when necessary, which wasn't often. The story was bad enough as it was. Out of the corner of my eye, I watched my sister suppressing a gag or two.

"So, what do you think?" I asked Dr. Marston. "What was going on with Lois? Was she crazy or what?"

Dr. Marston smiled slightly. "Crazy is not a word we like to use. But there are several things it could have been, although with what little information I have here, I hate to give a snap diagnosis."

"Go ahead," I said, "snap away."

"Not knowing the woman's history, it would be hard to say, but there are personality disorders that could account for this exaggerated change in personality, or even an obsessive-compulsive personality. If this were a recent change in behavior, severe depression could be the root problem. But what interests me most right now, Mr. Kovak, is your need to bring all this up at the dinner table."

I don't know how I would have answered that if the phone hadn't rung at that particular moment. Talk about saved by the bell. The call was from the station and by the time I got off, Dr. Marston was taking her leave.

"Well, Dr. Marston, it sure was nice meeting you," I said, "and thanks for the insight into my case. It's gonna help a lot."

She smiled. "I don't see how."

I didn't either, but I just shook her hand and opened the door for her. She and Jewel said their good-byes as I hightailed it up the stairs my sister couldn't navigate to hide in my room for the rest of the evening.

MONDAY MORNING at nine o'clock I was back on the Bell case with a vengeance when I got a call from Liaison Officer Leon Purdue.

"Deputy Kovak?" he asked.

"Yeah, how you doing, Officer Purdue?"

"Leon."

"Milt."

"Okay, Milt. Got some news for you. First off, let me read this back to you." And then he read me off the street address I'd given him that had been listed on the Bell's 1986 tax return.

"That's it."

"No, it ain't."

"What's that supposed to mean?"

"There is no such number on that street. The street stops about one hundred blocks short of that number."

"Well, that's interesting."

"Ain't it just?"

"Maybe they wrote it down wrong?"

"You got the tax returns, right?"

"Right."

"They got the same number on their W2s, the return, et cetera et cetera?"

I thumbed through the information on my desk. "Yeah."

"How many times is a body gonna write down his own address wrong?"

"Yeah. Got a point." I thanked him and hung up. Then I called information for Americus, Georgia, and tried to get the number of Martin Luther King, Jr. High School. Except there was no Martin Luther King, Jr. High School in Americus, Georgia. Then I called Atlanta information for a number for Jefferson Davis High School. Surprise, surprise. No such place.

And then it dawned on me. We didn't have a problem burying the Bell family, because there was no Bell family. Those bodies in the morgue were just a collected figment of the collective imagination. I sat back and reflected on my thoughts, smiling at my own wit. Till it struck me that there really were five bodies, three of 'em just babies, and somebody damn well better do something about that. The only somebody I could think of was me.

I didn't know a hell of a lot about the Witness Protection Program, but it stood to reason, in my way of thinking, that they wouldn't give them papers as phony as the ones I'd found. I mean, really, a phony address on IRS forms? High school diplomas for high schools that didn't exist? In my gut it was looking more and more like Bill Bell was on the lam from something and had taken his whole family down with him. Maybe that was why the house was in the shape it was in. Living with a man on the lam's gotta be bad on a lady's psyche.

At that point in my thinking, Dalton stuck his head through the door. "Milt, you got a visitor."

"Okay. Send 'em on in."

Dalton stepped aside and a man stepped through the door. He was about five eight, had dark hair receding a little worse than mine, wore his suit like a feed sack, but had what the ladies would call a disarming smile. "Chief Deputy?"

"That's me." I stuck my hand out to shake, which he did. He shook hands like his daddy had taught him a man oughta.

"I'm Jackson Taylor, with the U.S. Marshal's Office in Oklahoma City."

"Nice to meet you."

"My pleasure, my pleasure." He continued to pump my hand with one of his through the introduction, while with the other he slapped me on the back. Friendliest fed I'd ever met. I invited him to sit down in my one visitor's chair and took my swivel chair behind the desk.

"Reason I'm here, Chief Deputy, is the file you asked for from the FBI."

"Oh?" Now this was finally getting interesting.

"I got a call from Washington, you know how they are, asking if I'd come on down here and see what I could do to help you out."

"Help me out how, Marshal Taylor?"

"Well, with your interest in the file you were asking about."

"I only sent that in a couple of days ago. Never new the Fibbies to be so quick."

He grinned real big. "No big deal. I was in the neighborhood. Thought I'd just see what I could do to help you out."

"The information I requested was for an identity on some fingerprints I sent them."

"Uh-huh."

"You got that information?"

"Mind if I ask you a question first?"

I shrugged. "Suppose not."

"Why you want to know?" he asked, leaning toward me with a real earnest look about him.

"Sheriff's department business."

He leaned back, grinning, and held his arms out wide. "Hey, we're all just one big family, ya know? All us branches of law enforcement need to stick together."

"Okay. So, you got an ID on those prints?"

"Milt . . . can I call you Milt?"

"Sure, Jackson, go right ahead."

"Milt, you seen those spy movies where the spy says 'That's on a need-to-know basis'?"

"Yeah, I seen that."

"I hate to sound like a cliché—"

"Jackson, may I call you Jackson?"

"Of course!"

"Jackson—" I leaned across the desk, putting on my own earnest face, "I need to know."

"Why's that, Milt?"

"'Cause we got us a dead body."

He nodded his head a couple of times and stood up. "I take it you're trying to identify this stiff you got?"

"Yeah, all five of the stiffs."

He sat back down again. "Five?"

"Yeah. Mama stiff, Daddy stiff, and three little baby stiffs."

His face turned a little pale and he said, "Fuck," under his breath. Finally he cleared his throat and looked up at me. "What say you take me over to where these bodies are, Chief Deputy."

I nodded my head and led him out to my unmarked squad car and we drove silently over to Longbranch Memorial where the morgue was kept. Dr. Jim proudly showed off his wares while I stood by the door. I noticed Jackson's color never had come back right. He looked at the bodies, spending a longer time with Lois than with the others, then turned back to Dr. Jim.

"I want these released to me as soon as possible."

"Now hold on a goddamn minute," I said, leaving my perch by the door. "By what right do you think you're taking these bodies?"

All his earlier good-buddy bullshit seemed to have disappeared. "Right of the federal government, Deputy." I noticed he'd dropped the "chief" but decided to let it slide.

"I'd sorta like to know why in the hell the federal government is interested in the Bell family, Jackson. You wanna enlighten me?"

Ignoring me, he turned to Dr. Jim. "Doctor, I want these bodies ready to be shipped outta here tomorrow morning."

"You got a court order?" Dr. Jim asked, cleaning his fingernails with a scalpel.

"What?"

Doc glanced up from his fingers to look at Jackson Taylor. Very slowly, as if speaking to the deaf, he said, "Court...order.... You got a court...order?"

"I'll have one by the morning."

"Then in the morning I'll start getting them ready. After I've seen your court order. Might take a couple of days though. This is a small town and my staff's nothin' to brag about."

Marshal Taylor whirled around and stalked out of the morgue. I grinned at Dr. Jim and he grinned back. We might have our little squabbles, he and I, but there's nothing can pull two people together like sticking it to the federal government.

SIX

I BARELY GOT in the private entrance to the sheriff's department before I heard a bellow coming out of Elberry Blankenship's office.

"Milton? That you?"

"Yes, sir," I called.

"Get your ass in here."

I got my ass in there. He was leaning back in his swivel chair looking at me as I walked in. Not a good sign. "Yes, sir?"

He righted his chair and leaned his elbows on the desk top. "Milton." He shook his head. "Milton, damn it."

"Sir?"

"You know how much I despise the feds?"

"Ah...."

"You know how much shit they can cause this little county?"

"Elberry—"

"You know how long that Jackson Taylor can talk on one subject?"

"Sheriff—"

He stood up and walked to the door of his office. I followed. "I don't want that asshole in my office again, Milton. Understand?"

"Yes, sir."

"If you hafta, kill the sumbitch."

I grinned and left, getting to my office just in time to pick up my phone on the third ring. I identified myself and heard a low rumble. "Bastard Hunter won't go along with us."

"Pardon?"

"Nothing feebler in this world, Milt, than a feeble old man. And you can quote me."

It finally dawned on me I was being talked to by Billy Moulini. "You talked to Haywood?"

"What I just say, boy?"

"Yes, sir."

"Son of a bitch."

"Won't stick it out, huh?"

"Fucking asshole."

"You talk to Roy Munsky about his mama's place?"

"Yeah. He'll sell to us if we meet the price the condo time-share people are offering. Which is $350,000."

I sucked in air. "For that old place?"

"It's the key. Jennifer Creek runs right through the back of the place. Without that, them condo assholes won't have nothing."

I nodded my head, then remembered he couldn't see me and said, "Uh-huh."

"Can't find the owner of the place across from the Munskys'. Nobody knows where he is, except the condo people."

"Well, if we get the Munsky place, and you not selling and me not selling, seems like the whole thing's down the tubes, right?"

"They get Falls End, they can take the whole bottomland down there and do their thing," Moulini said.

"Yeah, but Mr. Moulini, that's all swamp."

"Ever hear of landfill, boy? Developers don't give a rat's ass how long the thing's gonna stand. Build the fucker, sell it, and let it fall on somebody else's head. I know how they think, boy. I done it enough times myself, but I'll be goddamned if I'm gonna let 'em do it to my fucking mountain!" He hung up.

I noticed then that even in the air-conditioning I was sweating like a pig. I didn't want them turning the mountain into a time-share condo project any more than Moulini did. I loved that mountain, and my house, and Jennifer Creek, and everything about that part of the county. It was my home now, home for my sister and her children. Damned if I was gonna let this go without a fight.

I sat about most of that day worrying, and that evening, on my way home, drove by the Bell house. The landlord had been on the horn bitching to the sheriff. He wanted to know when he could have his house back to rent to somebody else. That, of course, all depended on when we were through with it, and since I hadn't made it through one-quarter of the garbage yet, we could have a bit of a problem.

As I pulled onto Grapevine Road, I parked on the street in front of the house next door, remembering I never had talked to the other neighbor, Kathy Ann Hope. The idea of talking to Kathy Ann beat the hell out of digging through the garbage. Kathy Ann was the oral hygienist for my dentist, so I saw her professionally on occasion. She was also the daughter of my sister's best friend, Mavis Davis, so since Jewel Anne had come back home, I'd seen her more often on a social basis. She was divorced and had a two-year-old girl and a four-year-old boy. Kathy Ann would turn twenty in the spring.

I knocked on the door and waited while she came to open it. I could hear the kids screaming in the background. "Hey, Mr. Kovak, how are you?"

"Sorry to bother you so near supper, Kathy Ann, but I need to ask you some questions about the people next door."

She opened the door wider to allow my entrance. "I was wondering when in the hell you'd get around to that. Them people been dead for days now."

"Sorry. Been busy." I smiled at Kathy Ann. There was something about this little girl that I liked. I think it might have been that she had whatever it is that's the female equivalent of balls. She'd never been accused, and never would be, of being pretty; her face was too round, her nose too big, her teeth too small, her hair too coarse, for anybody to use that description. And in that way, she looked just like her mama. But she was lucky that looks wasn't all she'd inherited from Mavis. Mavis and Kathy Ann were the only two people I'd ever met who had an instant comeback for anything anybody said. While most of us go home and two days later think of some scathing remark that would have fit perfectly to whatever situation, Mavis or Kathy Ann would have come up with something ten times better in an instant. Get the two together, and you'd have to hold your gut laughing.

I guess Mavis and her husband, Bert, had the best marriage I'd ever been witness to. Where Mavis was outgoing, ready to take on the world, Bert was shy and retiring and would just as soon the world go jump itself, thank you very much. And between them they'd raised a hell of a kid.

Kathy Ann, like a lot of girls in small towns where the only real form of entertainment is getting laid in the backseat of somebody's car, got herself knocked up young, at the tender age of fifteen. But because the high school had a policy not allowing married students to attend, Kathy Ann went against convention and decided not to marry the boy. Instead, she decided to go on to school. Which was when I first got to know her.

The school district, in its wisdom, decided pregnant girls shouldn't be allowed an education, even though the rules of the school specified only married students. So Kathy Ann and her parents took it to court. Winning the suit was only the first part of the battle. Getting her through picket lines of angry, mob-crazy parents was my job. I escorted her to school every day for two weeks. By this time, she was six months pregnant, and I had to admit I felt pretty close to murder a few times when supposed adults would start throwing rocks at this little, pregnant child. The Kathy Ann Davis situation was the closest Longbranch ever got to a full-bore riot. And the town was torn in two over it for months. My wife and I fought about it on a regular basis. She couldn't see why Mavis and Bert didn't just pack Kathy Ann off someplace like proper parents would do. I remember at one point telling LaDonna she was a mean-minded, spiteful, petty little person. She cut me off for a month.

Mama was alive in those days. And every Sunday during Kathy Ann's pregnancy, Mama would wait outside the church for the Davis's to show up, link arms with Kathy Ann, and walk her into the sanctuary. She was a strange woman, my mama. Couldn't cook worth a damn but was the best seamstress I ever saw. Made the suit my daddy was buried in. If she'da been born in another time, another place, no telling what she could have been. She could make anything. Look at something and copy it. No matter what it was. She could draw pictures and paint and once, when I was little, she built me a castle like King Arthur's Court. Drawbridges and everything.

And she could shoot. The youngest of four girls, her daddy had decided that Dorthea was gonna be his son. He taught her to hunt and fish and dress her kill, and how to pull an engine out of a tractor. Though she admitted not liking the latter that much, what with the grease under her fingernails and all. But she was a better shot than either me or Daddy.

Every Christmas Mama had a thing about making arrangements out of mistletoe. Daddy would drive into the country till Mama found a tree dripping with the stuff and she'd get out of the car with her twenty-two and shoot down however much she wanted, snipping the stems as neatly as if it were done with garden shears. After Daddy died, I kept up the practice. She was shooting down mistletoe until she broke her hip at the age of seventy-nine.

And I do believe that if anyone at church had given Kathy Ann the least bit of grief while my mama was around, she'da put her cane under one arm and leveled her twenty-two at 'em with the other. But everybody at the First Baptist Church already knew: Don't mess with Dorthea Kovak. And with Mama and Mavis around, it went without saying, you don't mess with Kathy Ann.

Anyway, to make a long story longer, Kathy Ann went on to graduate high school, with a second bun in the oven. She and the first baby's father, Buddy Hope, had kept on keeping on, and got married two weeks after school was out, about three months before their little girl was born. A year later Buddy decided that making babies was a hell of a lot more fun than being a daddy, so he took off. Kathy Ann borrowed money from her folks to go to dental hygienist school in Tulsa, taking the kids with her, and came back six months later to a job and her own house. Jewel Anne had confided in me on occasion that Kathy Ann wouldn't take a penny off her folks and had already paid them back half of the money for school. You gotta admire a kid like that.

This was the first time I'd been in Kathy Ann's house. Taking money's not the same thing as taking furniture. Furniture is an entirely different thing. I noticed the couch looked familiar, like the one that used to be in Bert's den, and I remembered seeing Bert and Mavis at the furniture store the same time my wife and I were buying new carpet for our house buying the table that stood in Kathy Ann's dining room. She ushered me to an easy chair, got the kids sitting down at the table with full plates, and sat herself down while I eased myself into the easy chair.

"So, what do you want to know?" she asked.

"Anything. Everything. Specially next of kin."

She shook her head. "Robbie played some with their little boy, even though he was older. Only boys in the neighborhood. And I'd see the little girl sometimes. Didn't even know they had a baby till they'd been there well on six months. Kept to theirselves, ya know?"

"That's what I hear."

"Saw her more at the bank than I ever did around here, and her living right next door!"

"Same thing Mrs. Kirby said."

Again she shook her head. "Mrs. Kirby and me went in the house after ya'll got through with it. I couldn't believe it, Mr. Kovak. I mean it! Nastiest place I've ever seen in my life! All I could think of was them little kids living in that filth! Made my skin crawl!"

"You ever see anybody come visit?"

"No."

"The little boy ever mention a grandma, anything like that?"

"No. Sorry. I been waiting for you to come ask me questions and here I sit without a bit of information to give you."

"Not your fault, Kathy Ann. I just don't think there's any information to get."

As I got up to leave, she said, "You tell Aunt Jewel hidy for me, okay?"

I grinned. "Sure thing, honey. You take care now."

I walked across the lawn to the Bell house and started to use the key to let myself in the front door. Then I noticed the door was unlatched. And I got pissed off. Dalton was the last person over here, to my knowledge. Time that boy learned a few simple things about being a cop. I pushed the door open and stepped inside, just in time to see a figure run through the doorway into the kitchen.

"Hey!" I yelled. I took off after him, almost losing my balance in the shit on the kitchen floor, making me several yards behind as I ran out the back door.

I saw him vault over the chain-link fence in the backyard and head into the trees that bordered Grapevine Road from the back. On the other side of the line of trees was pasture-land. It took me a few minutes longer than the other guy to get over the fence, and by the time I did, he was just a distant figure practically to the other side of the pasture on his way to Hays Road half a mile away. I climbed back over the fence and hurried to my car, putting a call into the station as I started my engine and headed toward Hays Road. Jasmine Bodine, one of the night deputies, answered my call.

"Anybody out in a car right now, Jasmine?"

"Just you, Milt."

"Well, get somebody over to the south end of Hays Road by the power station. I'm coming up from the north end. Looking for a guy on foot. Blue jeans, red windbreaker, dark hair. Do it now."

"Yeah, Milt. Okay."

I drove slowly down Hays Road coming from the north end, looking on both sides of the road. There wasn't much to see. Just a couple of old farmhouses. He could be hiding in any of the outbuildings, I figured. I needed manpower. By the time I got to the power station, I had to wait another fifteen minutes for anybody to show up. Just my luck, it was Dalton.

He got out of his car all grins. "Hey, Milt."

I rolled down my window. "Jasmine tell you what we're looking for?"

"Yeah."

"You take the west side of the road, check houses and outbuildings, and I'll take the east."

"Okay."

I knew it was gonna be a fruitless search. The fifteen minutes I'd wasted waiting for Dalton would be enough for the perp to walk halfway to Tulsa if he had a good tailwind. But we went through the motions, disturbing a lot of folks at the supper table for absolutely nothing.

I went back to the station, telling Dalton he could go on home since that's where he was headed when Jasmine found him. I wrote up the incident quickly, drove back by the Bells' to make sure the house was locked up tight, then drove on toward my mountain.

All eighteen miles home all I could think about was why somebody would want to break into the Bells' house. With all the rumors running around the county about the condition of the house, I couldn't imagine any self-respecting burglar wasting his time. But why else would somebody be in the house? Then I had to wonder if Jackson Taylor was the only fed in the area and just how badly the feds wanted whatever information they wanted on the Bells.

As I pulled into the road leading to my house, I noticed a strange Cadillac parked next to the corral. Not that the Cadillac was all that strange, it was just that I didn't know anybody who owned one. The only person I could think of offhand who might own one was Billy Moulini, and the thought of him coming to visit scared the dog piss outta me.

But as I parked my car and got out, I saw the screen door of the front porch open and Jewel and a man come out. I walked up to them.

Jewel looked at me and blushed. "Harmon, you remember my brother, Milton?"

I shook hands with Harmon Monk. "Hey, Harmon, how you doing?" I asked.

"Fine, Milt, you?"

"Fine."

We all three stood there for a few minutes staring alternately at our feet and the sky.

"Well," Harmon said. "I gotta go." He looked at Jewel. "Bye, Jewel."

"Bye, Harmon."

He turned and walked off to his Cadillac with Jewel and me watching his every move. All I could think was it sure as hell took him long enough. Then, of course, I had to wonder if his wife knew he was up here. As the Cadillac turned and headed down our road to Mountain Falls Road, Jewel turned and headed into the house. I followed.

"What's for dinner?" I asked.

"Dinner?"

"You know, that meal that comes after lunch and before breakfast?"

"Oh." We were standing in the entry hall and she looked toward the kitchen like she expected it to tell her what to do.

"Where are the kids?" I asked, hoping to give her an easier question.

"Kids?"

"Your children."

"Oh. Ah, Marlene's over at Lacy's. And Carl and Leonard went to the mall."

I nodded. It wasn't really a mall. What we had in Longbranch was three stores and a video game arcade connected with covered walkways. But we called it a mall. Made us feel sophisticated.

I took Jewel's hand and escorted her into the living room and made her sit down on the sofa. "So," I said, taking my ease in my easy chair. "What Harmon have to say?"

"Nothing much."

"He drive all the way up here from Bishop just to admire our view?"

Jewel blushed. Didn't take much. She stood up. "I guess I'd better start dinner."

I followed her into the hallway to the phone. "Forget dinner. I'm gonna call Leonard at the video arcade and get him to pick us up a pizza, how's that sound?"

She nodded her head and kept walking to the kitchen. I picked up the phone and dialed the number for the video arcade and waited a few minutes while Leonard was rounded up and then I told him what to do.

"I spent all my money, Uncle Milt. I don't have enough to buy a pizza."

"That's the good thing about living in a small town, kid. Just tell Henry at the pizza place that you're my nephew and to put it on my bill. Just this once though."

I added the last as I envisioned twenty-seven large pizzas feeding every kid at the high school going on my bill. I hung up and went up to my room for a beer. I popped the top and laughed to myself at my sister's expense. Poor Jewel.

Harmon Monk had been her big heartthrob in high school. He was several years older than she and had dropped out of school. I'm not exactly sure how they met, but I sure knew all about them seeing each other. Mama was on the phone to me on a daily basis back in those days, letting me know what Daddy was thinking.

The upshot of all the thinking Daddy was doing was that Harmon Monk was trash and his little girl could do a hell of a lot better. And, in a way, given circumstantial evidence, I suppose you could say the boy was trash. He was raised by a drunken father on a pig farm outside of town. His mama was a shrunken, abused lady who barely spoke above a whisper. As I remembered it, there were twelve Monk children, Harmon being somewhere in the middle. I'd gone to school with one of the older Monks, a boy named Jesse, who'd ended up going to jail somewhere for something. Everybody thought that that was just about par for a Monk.

Daddy had finally put his foot down and forbidden Jewel to see Harmon. And Jewel being Jewel, she didn't sneak out or do anything but sit in her room and cry her eyes out about it. But Harmon, being a Monk, just made matters worse by driving by the house in his old jalopy and screaming Jewel's name. And getting drunk and banging on the front door of the house in the middle of the night. Daddy finally set the law on him. Which was me.

I went out to the pig farm, which was a pitiful place, a yard full of rusted cars and farm machinery and about a dozen scrawny-looking porkers. I put the fear of God into the boy, telling him that if he went around my sister again I'd throw him in jail. He got drafted shortly after that and went to Vietnam. And Jewel went to college.

It was years later that I discovered that Harmon had come back to Prophesy County, taking his now-dead daddy's pig farm and turning it into a car graveyard, and selling used parts on the side. Now he had eighteen junkyards and used car part stores all over this end of Oklahoma. And drove a brand-new Cadillac. And lived in a house on Junger Hill in Bishop, which is where the few rich people we got live. And of course, in that house also lived his wife and two daughters.

I had known, of course, from Glenda Sue, that Harmon had asked after Jewel Anne when she had her trouble down in Houston. I had half expected, when I brought Jewel back up here, to see Harmon sitting out front waiting for her. I figured it showed the guy had some kinda restraint to wait six months before visiting. Then I wondered if this was the first time he'd visited. Jewel Anne was alone most all the day, with the kids in school and me at work. Maybe this was just the first time I'd caught 'em. I thought maybe it was time I acted like a brother. A nosy brother. But then again, I thought, knowing my sister, I woulda known if somebody'd been around. Jewel was never good at lying, or even evading the truth.

I walked downstairs and knocked on the door to Jewel's room. After she said come in, I opened the door and went in. She was lying on the bed, staring at the ceiling.

"I saw Kathy Ann Hope today. She said to tell you hidy."

"That's nice."

"She's pregnant again."

"Uh-huh."

"By President Reagan."

"That's nice."

"Jewel Anne."

"Um."

I reached out and gently shook her arm. She looked up at me. "What?" It was an irritated "what."

"Did you hear a word I said?"

"About what?"

"Kathy Ann!"

"Who?"

"Jesus!" I threw up my hands and walked into the kitchen in time to hear Leonard's Volkswagen pull in. Leonard had picked up Marlene on his way home so all three kids came blasting in together. I set the table and Marlene fixed a salad and we ate salad and pizza, ignoring the fact that Jewel Anne didn't make it to dinner.

SEVEN

THAT TUESDAY MORNING, after I'd checked in at the station, I drove my unmarked squad car over to the Bell house to have another look around before the feds decided to burn the place down or whatever. It wasn't much cleaner than it had been. The smell was a little better because everything'd sorta dried up. I figured I was lucky it was autumn or the insects would be hell in the place. As it was, only the lowly roach stayed around to inspect the premises. Him and about three thousand of his brothers and sisters.

Because I'm a coward by nature, I decided to start again in the master bedroom, there being less stuff there to interest la cucaracha. I started by pulling out drawers in the dresser, going through each piece of clothing, looking at the bottoms of the drawers for anything taped there, looking inside the dresser walls itself for taped objects, and going through the whole pile of engineering magazines, page by page. Nothing there. I took the bed apart, looking under the mattress and along the mattress for any new-looking seams. Nothing.

Then I decided to tackle the piles of clothes, starting with the clean pile first, as was my nature. It
wasn't until I was halfway through the dirty pile that
I found something. In the pocket of a red flannel
bathrobe I found a small stack of receipts, three to be
exact. All with the address of the Vista Haven
Apartments on the shores of Lake Blue, for Unit 3,
and all in the amount of $185.00, and all dated on
the first of the month for the months of August,
September, and October, and all signed by Augustine Flowers, Manager. I sat back on my haunches
and stared at the damned things. A clue. Goddamn
it to hell and back if this wasn't a clue!

I got up off the floor as quick as my fifty-year-old
body would let me and, locking up the Bell house,
hopped into the squad car, and headed for Lake
Blue. Now to get to Lake Blue, you go like you're
going to Tulsa except you turn on Farm to Market
310 and then turn a bunch more. You sorta have to
know where you're going because the state never got
around to figuring Lake Blue was someplace anybody would look for. I personally hadn't been there
since the night of my high school graduation party,
which was in Longbranch at somebody's house. Afterward, though, me and Linn Robertson and about
nine other football players headed out to Lake Blue
with three cases of beer and four bottles of Jack
Daniels and proceeded to make ourselves sicker than
shit. Except me, of course. Oh, I drank everything

they handed me and eventually passed out—I just never got sick.

There's always been jokes about why the place is called Lake Blue. If the truth be known, if they'da been naming it after the color of the lake it woulda been called Lake Baby Shit Yellow. Linn Robertson always said it was named as it was because having that being the only lake around sure did make you blue. Of course, there was the theory that with all the parking going on around there, that it was named after blue balls, but I won't go into that.

It took me about forty-five minutes and a couple of U-turns before I got to the lake, then I had to go around the damn thing twice before I spotted the Vista Haven Apartments. I suppose I was looking for something a little bigger. The Vista Haven was a four-unit complex with a parking lot backing up to the water, now empty except for a motorcycle and a beat-up Honda Civic. I got out of the car and went in search of Augustine Flowers. None of the four units had "Manager" by the apartment number, so I finally just started pushing doorbells until somebody answered. The guy who answered looked more like he belonged to the motorcycle than the Civic. No shirt, tattoos, and lots of dirty hair. I asked him about Miz Flowers and was pointed in the direction of a house about two hundred yards from the complex. I thanked him kindly and wandered over in that direction. The house was what you might call generic house. It had no yard to speak off, just weeds, no shutters at the windows, no distinguishing marks whatsoever. Not even a washing machine on the front porch, which woulda been something, at least. I rapped on the door and a woman old enough to have dated God answered.

"What?"

"Excuse me, ma'am, I'm looking for Miz Augustine Flowers," I said, smiling like my mama taught me.

"Whatja want?"

"You Miz Flowers, ma'am?"

"So what if I am?"

I showed her the receipts I pulled out of my pocket.

"So what?"

I showed her my badge.

She looked real close at it and then at me. "That's for Prophesy County, asshole. This here's Tejas. You ain't got no call to come bothering me."

She slammed the door in my face. I went back to the fourplex and asked the biker if I could use the phone.

"Sure, man, come on in." He indicated the phone and sat back on the couch, picking up his beer and his joint to continue watching his soap opera.

I put my call through. When someone answered, I asked for Chief Deputy Bill Williams. That's when the biker got up, stubbed out the joint, and walked out the front door. Pretty as you please. And here I was, innocent as all shit.

I explained the problem to Bill, who's my counterpart in Tejas County, and he said he'd be over in a minute to have a little jaw with Miz Flowers.

I left the biker's apartment, locking up after me, and went to wait in the parking lot next to my squad car, surprised to find the motorcycle still in residence, but the Honda gone. And I was so sure. Just goes to show ya, I suppose. I stared out at the waters of Lake Blue, amusing myself by counting condoms floating on its greasy surface.

Bill's squad car showed up about fifteen minutes after my call. He got out and we shook hands.

"Shit, Milt, been awhile."

"That's the truth. How are you, Bill?"

"Fine, fine. Had me some prostate trouble awhile back, but doing fine now."

"Ain't that always the way?" I said. "Finally get old enough to figure out what to do with the damned thing and it goes haywire on ya."

Bill laughed. "I gotta tell you though, the doctor did talk about amputating it and sending it to the Guinness people."

"That small, huh?"

"Big, man, that big!"

We laughed like idiots and then got down to business. "Whatja need to see the old bat about anyway, Milt?"

"You heard about our suicide thing over in Prophesy?"

"Yeah, that bank lady and her whole family. Heard about that."

"Well, I found these receipts"—I showed them to him—"in their house. Wanted to check it out. But Miz Flowers slammed the door in my face. Suppose I shoulda reported to you first."

He gave me one of them looks, but didn't say "Yeah, you should have, asshole," because we're sorta friends.

"Well, come on," he said, "let's go give Miz Flowers some shit."

She was about as friendly as before but a little more cooperative. She wouldn't go over to the fourplex to let us in, but she gave us the keys. As we were walking back toward the fourplex, we heard one of the radios of one of the squad cars start squawking.

We walked over to the cars and found out it was Bill's. After about half a minute, he started up his engine and called over his shoulder to me, "Got a wreck over on the highway. You go ahead. Just take them keys back to Miz Flowers when you're through."

I waved my thanks and watched him pull out of the parking lot, siren screaming. When I was a young deputy, I thought that was the fun part of the job, but now, all that screeching just gives me a headache.

I used the key and opened the door of Unit 3. I'm not sure what I was expecting, but this wasn't it. It was a one-bedroom apartment with a balcony overlooking the lake. The carpet, which belonged to the unit, was old and stained and a little threadbare. But that was the only thing old, stained, and threadbare in the place.

The apartment looked like a layout in *Bride's Magazine*. Most of the carpet was covered with a new, pale-blue rug. Everything was new and shiny and done in shades of pale peach and light blue. The sofa was a floral design of those two colors with throw pillows of both colors resting on it, and there were two wingback chairs of baby blue. The coffee table was a big square butcher block with a flower arrangement mainly of peach and blue flowers. The walls were painted peach and had pictures that followed the color scheme, and the towels in the kitchen had little peach-colored rosebuds on 'em.

The bedroom rug covering the carpet was white on white with a nubby design of some sort. The double bed was covered in a white eyelet spread with more peach-and-blue throw pillows. The curtains were lacy and clean. The bathroom was immaculate, with blue bath mats, a floral peach-and-blue shower curtain, peach-and-blue towels, little wicker baskets covered in lace, some holding peach-and-blue soap balls and some with little peach-and-blue flowers. Hell, even the toilet paper was peach.

I opened the closet door and looked inside, expecting lots of peach-and-blue clothing. It was almost that bad. Hanging in the closet were several white nighties, all lacy, frilly things, a couple of real feminine-looking sundresses, and some men's clothes. All pale colors, lightweight sweater-type pullovers, and a man's silk dressing gown, in burgundy and black yet. Like a bad thirties' movie. I pulled out the dressing gown and realized Bill Bell would have had a hard time getting the thing around his ample beer belly. Hence, the dressing gown didn't belong to Bill Bell.

In the dresser drawers I found more clothes. Lacy white and pale pink panties and teddies, old-fashioned stockings and a lacy garter belt, etc., etc. And a box with a diaphragm in it. In "his" drawer, I found skimpy little macho briefs in multicolors and a vibrator. In the bedside table, I found a bottle of Kama Sutra Oil and a copy of *The Rubaiyat of Omar Khayyam*. It didn't take me too long to figure out that maybe Lois Bell had a little something going on the side. Now I just had to wonder who all the "his" stuff belonged to.

I went through every article of men's clothing, checked inside and outside of every drawer in the apartment, but couldn't find anything to indicate "his" identity. Finally I left the apartment, locking up behind me, and strode over to Miz Flowers. Giv-

ing her back the key, I asked, "Can you tell me anything about the people who rented that unit?"

"No people. Just her."

"What was her name?"

"Alexandra Kincade."

Sounded like the name of a romance writer. But
somehow, it fit the personality of the interior de-
signer of the little love nest.

"There was a man staying there with her. Can you
tell me anything about him?"

"Didn't see no man. If I'da had, I'da charged
more for the apartment. That's a one-person rental
she was gettin'."

"Ever see any cars in the parking lot that didn't
belong?"

"What you think? I stand around my window all
day staring at them people? I don't give a flying fig
what any of them bunch do long's they pay the rent.
Are you through?"

"Just about, ma'am."

"Well, I'm through." And she slammed the door
in my face. Such a nice lady.

Actually, I really was through. If she didn't see the
man, or wouldn't admit it, there weren't any more
questions to ask. I went back to the squad car and
drove back to Prophesy County.

I drove immediately to the Bell house, to see what
else I could see. From my brief examination, just
more filth. Anything could be in there. I'd found the

receipts, hadn't I? But the thought of digging
through all that garbage was just too much to bear.
It was getting close to quitting time, so I locked up
the house and started driving back to the station.
Less than a block from the Bells' house, I passed a
car. A bright yellow Karmann Ghia. And sitting at
the wheel was Neville Crouch, Lois Bell's daughter's first-grade teacher. Less than a block from
Lois's house. I wondered why in the world he was
there. And wondered if maybe he might just be
looking for something. Like maybe receipts? He
glanced my way, recognized me, and after a brief
pause, waved. I waved back, watching in the rearview mirror as he passed Lois's house and kept on
going. I figured Neville Crouch and I might want to
have a little chat.

THAT NIGHT IT CAME a gully washer, rained like a
cow pissing on a flat rock. I sat in my windowed
room, swilling my beer, and watched the rivers form
in my backyard, hoping it would wash away some of
the leaves so I wouldn't have to rake.

There's something about a storm that really gets to
me. I guess it's the drama of it all. It's thrilling, ex-
citing, and depressing all together. Depressing, and
thrilling, for one, because mankind, such as it is,
can't do a damn thing about it. We can't make it
come and we can't make it go away. Depressing, too,
because you know it's got to end.

Nobody is indifferent to a storm. It either scares the dog piss out of you or makes you all aquiver. Personally, I just get all aquiver. A good storm gives promise, washing the slate clean, new beginnings. You're excited, never knowing what it might do next. Does this one have a tornado in it? Hail? Can you trust the weatherman? Oh, my, yes, I love a good storm. And this one was a doozy. Lightning, thunder, torrential downpour.

It woulda been fine if Jewel hadn't called up the stairs every fifteen seconds wanting to know if maybe we should take the kids to the storm cellar. The girl'd been out of Oklahoma too long. Couldn't remember we didn't get tornados in the fall. Much.

She hadn't talked any about Harmon Monk and neither had I. I figured she was a big girl now and I'd stuck my nose in her love life maybe once too often. We also didn't talk anymore about our problems, hers and mine, and she didn't, thank you very much, mention a repeat of our little dinner with the shrink. The fact that I stayed in my room on the second floor whenever possible, up the stairs she couldn't maneuver, might have had something to do with the fact that we were getting along so well.

Anyway, I could hear her downstairs most of that stormy night, and, in my mind's eye, I could see her laying out storm candles according to size and color, dusting the batteries in the flashlights, and filling sterilized milk jugs with water. Just in case.

THE NEXT DAY WAS COLD. Our first real cold spell, ushered in by the storm of the night before, no doubt. The temperature was in the fifties and the windchill was around thirty, but if you stayed where the sun shone, it was tolerable. Around ten o'clock that morning, Gladys rang me to say I had a call.

"Who is it?"

"Some lawyer named Task."

"Tell him I'm not here."

"You asking me to lie?" Gladys was real big on things like not lying and not stealing and not cheating and such. Admirable qualities in a sheriff's department clerk. Generally.

"Gladys, soon as I hang up this phone, I'm walking out the back door. So it won't be a lie." I hung up and sat back in my swivel chair and surveyed the ceiling. I didn't want Task calling me. I didn't want him wanting my house and land. I didn't want anybody wanting to build a time-share condo on my mountain. I also didn't want to get involved, but I supposed I was gonna have to.

I put in a call to Billy Moulini in Oklahoma City, charging it to my home number. I'm also kinda big on not cheating and not stealing. But lying—well, hell, that's practically part of my job description.

When he finally came on the line it was with the greeting, "Shit, boy, I don't like this."

"Me neither. I just got a call from Task, that damned lawyer."

"All lawyers be damned, Milton, they're nothing but a bunch a' pimps. Look, the county commissioners are meeting this week. You know I used to be one of them bunch?"

"Yes, sir."

"Well, I still know where a lot of dead bodies are buried, son—that's just a figure of speech."

"Yes, sir."

"So, you and me are gonna show up at that meeting and kick a little county ass. How's that sound?"

Actually, it sounded like fun. "Sounds fine, Mr. Moulini."

"'Bout time you called me Billy."

"Yes, sir."

"I'll call ya."

And he hung up. So now all I had to worry about was Lois Bell. Which was why I'd called Billy in the first place, so I wouldn't have to think about Lois Bell. Sometimes, I think what I'd really like to do is take an early retirement and go fishing every day. The only problem there, of course, is I don't like to fish and I don't like to eat fish. But I figure if I put my mind to it I could work around that.

But in thinking about Lois Bell, I started making lists of what I actually knew.

1. Bill and Lois Bell weren't really Bill and Lois Bell.
2. Neither one of them came from Georgia.

3. They never lived on Hazel St. in Oklahoma City.

4. Bill Bell's real initials were DT and he had been a captain in the Marine Corps.

5. Lois Bell's real initials were AT (née J) and she had worked in banking before, no matter what her résumé said.

6. Lois Bell had been having an affair in a rented apartment on Lake Blue with person or persons unknown. (Person probably. I couldn't see Lois Bell getting any kinkier than Kama Sutra oil and a vibrator myself.)

7. Lois died with a knot on her head from some still unknown cause.

8. Neville Crouch, who was connected to Lois by way of her daughter, had been seen lurking in the vicinity of the house. Well, maybe not exactly lurking, but...

9. The Justice Department was interested, which meant that Lois or Bill Bell or both either were wanted for something pretty heavy, or for some reason had been put under the wing of the Federal Witness Protection Program along with their family.

10. And this one was where I came in: There had to be family members out there somewhere who would want to see their kin

properly buried. Two families somewhere in America one with the initial *T* and one with the initial *J.* Somehow, I didn't think the library phone books would do me much good

I figured it was time I had a talk with Mr. Crouch. First, though, I looked up his address in the phone book, to make sure he didn't live anywhere near Lois. He didn't. Then I called the school, asked for Mrs. Oshley, and told her it was important that I speak with Mr. Crouch sometime that day. She told me his off period started at eleven and lasted through lunch until 1 P.M. I told her I was on my way, if she'd kindly have Mr. Crouch waiting somewhere quiet where we could talk.

I ENTERED the small conference room and looked at Neville Crouch, his tall, thin body, his dark curly hair, and wondered if he'd get suspicious if I asked him to turn around so I could see his back. Probably, I figured. We shook hands.

"What can I do for you, Chief Deputy?"

I smiled. "Just needed to ask a few more questions, Mr. Crouch."

"Shoot," he said, settling back in a chair, tipping the front feet off the floor, and stretching his legs.

"You mentioned when we talked before that you knew Mrs. Bell from the bank. That right?"

He nodded his head. "Yeah. Saw her every time I deposited my paycheck."

"How come you went in the bank instead of using the drive-in windows?" I asked. I never use the drive-in windows myself, but my reasons are totally innocent. I lost one of my '55's side mirrors doing that one time, never done it since.

"Because I usually bike to the school. I used to use the drive-in windows, but the security guard told me I couldn't anymore. That was about a year ago."

"Why's that?"

He shrugged. "I don't know. Why don't you ask him?"

"You didn't ask him how come?"

He sat up in his chair. "As a matter of fact I did. He said it was a rule. I let it go. I was mad, but what could I do? And why are you asking me these questions?"

"You know the Lake Blue area?"

Again, he shrugged. "I'd been out there. Once. When I first came to Longbranch. But it's not a place I'd go to again. Why?"

"When you went in the bank all those times, having your paycheck cashed, you and Miz Bell talk a lot?"

He shrugged. I was beginning to worry he'd get a crick in his neck. "Some."

"What about?"

He stood up. "Why? Why are you asking me all these questions? Am I under suspicion of something or what?"

"Goodness, Mr. Crouch, they're just questions. Trying to get a handle on Miz Bell is all. What did you two talk about?"

My aw-shucks bullshit didn't settle him down much, but he did answer. "The weather. The school. Her daughter. That's all."

"You two ever decide sometime maybe to have lunch together or something?"

His pasty complexion was turning a tomato red. "No. We never had lunch together. What is this bullshit?"

What a way for a teacher to talk, huh? I shrugged. Lot of that going around. "Like I said, just trying to get a handle on Miz Bell."

"I've got papers to grade and government reports to fill out. That's what I do during my off period. Not have lunch with my children's parents. So if you don't mind, Deputy." He took the two steps to the door of the conference room and opened it, ushering me out with one long thin arm.

"Thank you for your time, Mr. Crouch. And, oh, by the way"—and Lord, did I wish I had me a crumpled raincoat—"what were you doing yesterday over by the Bell house?"

"What?"

"When I saw you driving by. On Grapevine Road. Right by the Bell house. What were you doing?"

He looked at me long and hard and finally said, "None of your fucking business."

I tsk-tsked at the language and went on out. I got back to the station in time to sit down and do some thinking. Long hard thinking. I liked Neville Crouch for the Lake Blue "his," but what did it mean, even if he was "his"? Did it mean I had me a killer teaching little, innocent first graders? Or just an adulterer with bad taste in clothes?

The only concrete fact I had about the Bells was the birth of their last child, eighteen months before, in Oklahoma City. That one was probably true. But if they'd given the hospital the same phony address they'd given the IRS (and who in their right mind gives the IRS a phony address?), then I was still back at square one. I went through my files and pulled out the note on where I'd called the hospital once before. At that time I'd talked to a clerk who said my request had to be in writing. This time, when the switchboard operator answered, I asked for the office of the hospital administrator. I told him the whole story, told him how important it was that I have the information he had now, rather than waiting for the mails, told him he'd have a friend for life in Prophesy County, Oklahoma, and, when that didn't work, told him I knew somebody on the state hospital licensing commission who'd just love to spend about three weeks going over his hospital from stem to stern. The implied threat did the job. I got the address. The same one as the IRS had. I hung up, and I sat there with my head in my hands, my elbows on the desk, wishing I'd stayed a used car salesman.

And that's when the case decided to break a little, and it decided to do that only because of what they call the fourth estate. The great American press. Gladys knocked on my door, stuck her head in, and said, "You got you another visitor, Milton."

"If it's that damned lawyer I'm not here."

"It's not."

"If it's Jackson Taylor, tell him I died."

"It's not."

"Then who the hell is it?"

She stood up straight and got that look on her face and I knew I'd gone too far. You just don't curse in front of, and especially at, Gladys.

"Sorry, Gladys," I said.

She left the door open and walked off without a word or a backward glance. And I sat there wondering how she'd word the complaint she was gonna turn in to the sheriff. Half a second later a man entered. He was tall, over six feet, lean to the point of being skinny, had black hair with streaks of gray, worn longer than I've seen since the sixties, and skin of an unhealthy pallor. He was wearing Hush Puppies, faded blue jeans with a slight bell at the bottom, a faded red T-shirt with the legend "Eschew Obfustation" in dirty white, and an army field jacket with the insignias ripped off. Somehow, the outfit didn't go with his over-forty face.

I stood up. "Can I help you?" I asked.

"You Milton Kovak?"

"Yeah. And you're?"

"Marv Bernblatt, *Washington Post*." He didn't offer his hand and I didn't either. I motioned him to the visitor's chair, which he sank into, his long legs stretching out under my desk. Into my territory. My space. I shuffled my feet a bit, hitting one of his. He didn't budge. I moved my foot. I have no prejudice against Yankees. I really don't. Long as they know their place and don't get uppity. This one could become a problem in a hurry.

"What can I do for you, Mr. Bernblatt?"

"You the officer in charge of the murder-suicide?"

"Yeah."

"Tell me about it."

"Well, for one thing, it's being listed as a suicide-accident. No murder involved at this time."

"Yeah. Right."

"It already got wrote up in the local paper. Why don't you go check with them? And why would the *Washington Post* be interested?"

"I've seen your local rag. I came to you for the real skinny."

"You got some ID? Saying you're with the *Post?*"

He finally moved his feet and straightened up in his chair. "Actually, I'm free-lance. But the *Post* has shown some interest in this story."

"Shit." I stood up. "Look, I don't have time for this, Bernblatt. Why don't you go on now, okay?" I walked around the desk and showed him the door.

He stood up and walked to the door. Turning back, he said, "I thought all that shit in the movies about you southern hick cops being so stupid was an exaggeration. This is not the first time I've been proven wrong."

"If you're not outta this buildin' in two minutes, I'm jailing you for something, boy." He grinned and left, and I wondered why my accent, such as it was, had gotten thicker.

I didn't think any more about Bernblatt and that evening, as it was Wednesday, I went over to the Longbranch Inn, as is my custom. Every Wednesday night I eat dinner at the Longbranch, mainly because Glenda Sue gets off at eight o'clock and then we have the rest of the evening together. Since we hadn't seen each other since the Friday night before, when I'd left her smiling and happy, I figured tonight we could just go straight home.

I always sit at one of Glenda Sue's tables on Wednesday nights, and it's not just because she doesn't expect me to tip her. I sit there because that way I get to talk to my lady love every once in a while. So, that Wednesday night I sat down at my

usual table and Glenda Sue brought me over a quart
jar of iced tea, which is the way they serve iced tea at
the Longbranch Inn. I sat and sipped my tea and
waited for my usual Wednesday night repast: chicken
fried steak with cream gravy, mashed potatoes and
fried okra, with corn bread to sop with and peach
cobbler to help the digestion. And let me be the first
to tell you that the Longbranch Inn in Longbranch,
Oklahoma, makes the best damned chicken fried
steak in the whole country, Texas be damned. Every
time I've had to go to that damned state I've been
somewhere to eat where they claim to have the best
chicken fried steak in Texas. Well, that may be, but
compared to the Longbranch Inn's, it's nothing but
dog food.

So, anyway, I sat there sipping my iced tea, having daydreams about the feast to come, when over to
my table walks Marv Bernblatt, pretty as you please.
I looked up and saw him looming over me.

"Can't a man even eat in peace?"

"Hi, Deputy, how's it going?" He pulled out a
chair and sat his long body down.

"I don't remember inviting you to sit."

"Thanks, don't mind if I do."

"If that's what passes in D.C. for humor, no
wonder we're in so goddamned much trouble."

"Man, we need to talk."

"I already told you, boy, I ain't got nothing to tell you." For some reason I found myself imitating Rod Steiger in *In the Heat of the Night*.

"But I'm willing to trade."

"What you got I might be interested in?"

"The real names of the Bell family? Would that interest you?"

Well, he got me there. Yeah, you might say I was interested. But I got to hand it to me, I kept my cool. "Could interest me a might. What do you want, though?"

"Everything you got."

"Hardly seems fair."

"If you're willing to shake on it, I'll tell you everything I have, which is a hell of a lot more than just their names, if you let me see your files."

I thought about it. For a split second. I held out my hand and we shook, just as Glenda Sue brought my plate. "Honey," I asked her, "you got some paper around here and a pen?"

"Sure, be right back."

One bite of chicken fried steak later, I had pen and paper in hand. "Okay," I said between mouthfuls, "shoot."

"Her name is Annette Jacobsen Tapp. Two *p*'s. Husband David Robert Tapp. Both of them born and raised in Raleigh, North Carolina."

"Okay."

"He was an engineer for the Warrick Corporation. She was working as a bookkeeper for a small-time wheeler-dealer named Eddie Cowan. Mainly working on his legit books. But somehow she stumbled on some of his other enterprises—namely a deal he was into with some not-so-nice gentlemen from Colombia. Eddie was only a go-between, setting up the action for some local hotshots and the south-of-the-border types. Somehow, Annette was able to get the names of the locals involved. She turned the whole thing over to the feds, being the good little citizen type, fingered the bunch of 'em in court, because they'd been coming into Eddie's place for meetings during the day and Annette had taken them coffee on a number of occasions. Because of threats made by Eddie himself, Annette and her family were offered the Witness Protection Program. That was four years ago."

"So you think this Eddie Cowan found her and offed the whole family?"

"Not likely. Eddie Cowan was knifed in prison by a Colombian three days after he got there. He died a week later."

"So? What?"

"So I don't know. Got any Hispanics around here?"

"We got Indians and we got rednecks. No Colombians."

"What were they doing here anyway?"

"What do you mean?"

"According to your local rag, the family had only been here about a year."

"Yeah?"

"Where were they before that?"

"Their last baby was born in Oklahoma City. Why?"

"Because it's very unusual for the Witness Protection Program to place a family in a small town like this. They usually go for the big cities. More anonymity that way. And if they had them placed in Oklahoma City, why'd they move them here?"

"Got a question of my own."

"Okay." Bernblatt leaned back in his chair, obviously enjoying the role he was playing of adviser to the hick cop.

"If they were in Oklahoma City as the Bell family under the program, why would they put a phony address on their IRS form?"

"What?"

"On their IRS form. While they were in Oklahoma City. The address they put on there is the same address they gave to the hospital when the baby was born. There's no such number on that street."

"Interesting."

"How so?"

"Well, the WPP is tied in with all other branches of government. Not that any of the other branches know what the WPP is doing, it's just that certain names are not to be audited, et cetera. For instance, when you sent those prints to the FBI, a flag went up on their computer and the request was immediately turned over to the U.S. Marshal's Office.''

"How'd you know about that?"

"Why the hell do you think I'm here? I've got big ears. The better to hear all the plots with."

"Okay, so back to my original question: Why would they put a phony address on their IRS forms?"

"They wouldn't. If they were still under the cover of the WPP."

"What do you mean, still?"

"I'm beginning to think maybe they got dumped."

"You're losing me."

"Okay, listen." He leaned forward, elbows on the table, almost knocking over my iced tea. I moved it. "The Tapps—or Bells or what have you—got put under WPP protection because of possible reprisals from Eddie Cowan. Then, only a couple of months after she testifies, Eddie's dead. WPP, with their very limited brainpower, figures the Tapps no longer need protection. So they dump them. It's beginning to look to me as if the Tapps have been on the loose for over three years. Probably running from the Colombians."

"You think the Colombians found them? Here in Longbranch?"

"Yeah. That's what I think."

"I don't know much about the Colombian drug types, just what I see on *Miami Vice,* really, but would the suicide-accident be their MO?"

Bernblatt sat back in his chair and looked thoughtful. Or like he needed to go to the bathroom. I couldn't tell which. "You're right. Those types have never been known for their subtlety." He shrugged. "But who else could it be?"

I finished off the peach cobbler, sat back, and belched into my napkin like a gentleman. "Well, come by the office tomorrow and I'll show you my files."

"Tomorrow? No way, man. Tonight."

Glenda Sue came out of the back room where she'd changed into her street clothes, her purse hanging on her arm. "You 'bout through, Milt?"

I stood up and picked up my check. "Yeah, I'm through. See you in the morning, Bernblatt."

"Come on, man. We had a deal!" He was turning red in the face. I knew he was right. I also knew how much trouble I'd be in if Glenda Sue had to find her own way home.

Turning to my lady love, I said, "Honey, you mind if we stop by the station for a minute? Won't take long."

"Make any difference if I do mind?" She was not taking this well.

"Hey, Glenda Sue," a trucker called from a booth near my table, "I'll take you home!" He laughed like an idiot.

"See the trouble you're getting me into here, Bernblatt?"

"We have a deal."

"Honey..." I said to Glenda Sue, giving it my all. I tried giving quick introductions, which the light of my life ignored.

"Come on," she said, and led the way out the door.

EIGHT

WE SPENT THE BETTER PART of an hour with Bernblatt going over my files on the case. I spent my time watching Bernblatt. Glenda Sue spent her time staring daggers at my back. After he'd finished, he closed the file and looked at me.

"You don't have much here," he said.

"I never said I did."

"I gave you more than you gave me."

"Them's the breaks."

"You owe me."

"I don't owe you jack shit."

We glared at each other for a while until Glenda Sue broke the silence. "Are we ever getting out of here?"

"Yeah, honey," I said, "we're on our way."

"Just a goddamn minute—" Bernblatt started.

"No, you wait just a goddamn minute!" I said. I was getting hot. "We had a deal. You'd tell me what you have, I'd show you my files. For all I know you got a hell of a lot more than you told me. I took you on faith. I never told you I had much of anything. You just assumed it. And you know what assume does."

"What?"

"Makes an 'ass' out of 'u' and 'me.'"

"Gee, that's really funny." Bernblatt wasn't smiling.

"You want funny, go to Las Vegas."

"Now what?"

"Now my lady friend and I are going to her place. See ya." I walked toward the door, holding it for Glenda Sue and Bernblatt.

"That's not what I meant," Bernblatt said.

I locked up my office, waved good-bye to the night deputies, and ushered the troops out the side door. "I suppose you mean," I said to Bernblatt, resting my bottom against the driver's door of my '55, "what do I do next on the case?"

"Yeah. What do we do?"

"What's this 'we' shit? I don't recollect having a turd in my pocket."

"You know, you really should go on Carson, man. You're really hilarious." I glared at him and he glared at me. "You know what's going to happen next, don't you?"

"What's that, O wise Yankee asshole?"

"Jackson Taylor's going to step all over this. He's going to yank this case right out from under you, bury those bodies where no family member will ever be able to visit, and act like the Tapps vanished into thin air."

"That's a possibility."

"So what do you plan on doing to stop him?"

"Me? Stop the federal government? Yeah, right."

Bernblatt grinned. "Yeah, looks like those pants you're wearing haven't got room for balls big enough for that."

"Son, is that a challenge of some sort?"

Bernblatt shrugged. "Challenge, nudge, whatever you need it to be."

"Well, I don't see where the size of my family jewels got anything to do with this here."

"You're just going to let Taylor walk off with this?"

I sighed. I suppose I owed him. "Taylor's hands are tied for the moment at least. The county coroner's put a hold on the bodies for a little while. He's trying to give me time to find the next of kin."

"So now you know the next of kin."

"You got names and addresses?"

"Yep."

I sighed long and hard, knowing what I had to do. "You got a car?" I asked.

"Yeah. A rental. Why?"

I stuck my head in the driver's side of the '55. Glenda Sue was sitting in the passenger side, madder than spit. "Honey, why don't you take the car on to your place? I'll have Marv here give me a ride over there when we're through. Okay, honey?"

Glenda Sue slid across the bench seats and grabbed the key ring out of my fingers. "The keys will be in the ignition," she said. "Don't wake me when you drive off." She started the car and burned rubber my tires badly needed getting out of the parking lot.

"Touchy, isn't she?" Bernblatt said.

I didn't hit him. "You got me in more trouble than I need to be, that's for damn sure."

"Women, fuck 'em," Bernblatt said, heading back toward the side door.

I didn't say that had been my plan all along.

Once back inside my office, we made the calls, two of 'em, one to Mrs. Jacobsen, Lois's mama, and the other to Mr. and Mrs. Tapp, the parents of Bill Bell. Mr. and Mrs. Tapp were pissed off at just the possibility we might be trying to get them to foot the bill for the burial.

Mrs. Jacobsen, on the other hand, took it pretty hard. She asked about her grandchildren and when I told her, her pain was only trebled by the fact that there had been a new baby she hadn't even known about. She thought she could borrow the money from her son, Lois's brother, to come down and collect the bodies.

"I'm really sorry to have to be the one to tell you this, Miz Jacobsen," I said.

"I don't envy you your job, young man" was all she said before she hung up.

Bernblatt and I sat there staring at each other for a while. Finally he broke out in a big grin. He could afford to. He hadn't been the one talking to Mrs. Jacobsen.

"Well, that's it," he said.

"That's what?"

"We got Taylor by the proverbial balls."

"There is that."

"No way in hell he can touch those bodies now."

"There is that."

"The story's got to come out now."

I shook my head. "That's all this is to you, huh? A story?"

He leaned back in his visitor's chair, stretching his long legs out before him. His face had a thoughtful—but ugly—expression on it. "Maybe three years ago this was just a story. But not anymore. This is more than a story, Deputy. A lot more."

I nodded my head, hating to agree with him but having to. "Yeah. This is more than just another case to me, too."

"Why?"

I shook my head. "The babies? Hell, I don't know. I want to say because I knew Lois. But that ain't it. Anybody ends up dead in this county, chances are I knew 'em." I thought some more, then said, "Did you see the house?"

Bernblatt nodded his head.

"I think maybe...maybe that's the thing. For a woman like Lois to live like that...to raise her children like that.... I'm not a shrink. I don't pretend to be. But something was mightily wrong in that house." I straightened up in my chair and looked out the window at the black night sky. "The lady next door said it was evil. Pure and simple evil." I laughed. "Guess that'll give you something to laugh about when you get back."

"No, man. I know what you're saying. I took some psych courses along the way. A woman like Annette—Lois. I saw the house they left behind in Raleigh—nice little tract home. Reminded me of my mother's apartment in Brooklyn. Could eat off the floors, man, that kinda clean. For her to change that much there had to be some heavy stuff going on. For both of them. David changed, too. Man, he was an engineer. Worked for the same company for five years, and before that a marine officer. Then the shit hits the fan. Think about it. Think what it would do to you if your old lady got in trouble bad enough that the family had to split—live in hiding for the rest of your life. Change your name, change your kids' names. Man, that's heavy shit right there."

"What do you make of his folks, though? The way they acted when I called them?"

He shook his head, and we both sat there for a while, thinking to ourselves about the awfulness of it all. And I got to wondering what would make folks act that way about their own blood? The fruit of their loins, so to speak? Now, I don't have any children myself, but I couldn't think of anything, say,

Leonard, my nephew, could do that would make me not want to bury his body. I mean, even if he turned out to be a mass murderer and died in the electric chair, still I'd bury him. Maybe not next to Mama, maybe not even in the same cemetery, but somewhere. That's what family's all about.

Finally I swiveled around toward Bernblatt. "You wanna give me a ride over to Glenda Sue's?"

He pulled his long frame out of the chair. "Yeah, what the fuck."

I looked at him for a moment. "Ya know, I knew a guy down in Houston used to use that word in every sentence."

"What word? Fuck?"

"Yeah. He was a real irritating asshole."

He bowed low from the waist. "I'm sorry if I've offended your sensibilities, Deputy."

I grinned and slapped him on the back. "No problem. Just don't want you turning into a more irritating asshole than you already are."

He dropped me off at Glenda Sue's trailer house, which was dark, with all the curtains drawn and the lights off. I don't need much more of a hint than that. I started the '55 and drove to my mountain.

As I turned into the driveway, the beeper went off. I pulled up in front of the house and went into the darkened living room for the phone. I listened a moment to the silence of the house, listening to the little noises that let me know all was well. The creaking of a bed, the not-so-gentle snore coming from my younger nephew's room. I picked up the phone and dialed the sheriff's department.

When A.B. identified himself I said, "Hey, A.B., it's Milt. You rang?"

"Milt, you need to come back to the station?"

"I just left."

"Well, we got some trouble?"

"What kind of trouble?"

"Kind I can't go into on an open phone?"

"Shit, A.B., what's going on?"

"Milt, you come on to the station, okay? Before I put the cuffs on Jasmine."

"What?"

"See ya."

He rang off, leaving me alone in my darkened living room wondering what in the hell was going on down at the station. I went back out, locking the door behind me, and headed back toward Longbranch. Jasmine Bodine was one of our deputies. She worked mostly nights, but this week had been pulling days for a special project of the sheriff's. Jasmine was one of those people ill-suited to carry their own name, because her name was the only thing fresh and pretty about her. She was one of those people who life had dealt with badly, mainly by her marrying Lester Bodine, who spent his evenings with every other woman in town while his wife was working. Since she'd been with the sheriff's department,

Lester had had two paternity suits filed against him. Why she stayed with the man no one knew.

I got to the station and pulled into my parking space. Even from there I could hear the screaming from inside. Once inside it was overwhelming. The place was crowded. Jasmine sat at a deputy chair with a strange little smile on her face. Just sat there quietly amid all the noise. The noise was coming from her loving husband, who was shouting "I want her locked up! I want her hung! I want her skin peeled off her body!"

Some more of the noise was coming from the two ambulance attendants who were trying to get Lester on the gurney. And I could see why. He was all over blood from his waist to his knees.

I walked up to Jasmine and gently stood her up and led her to my office, with Lester screaming at us both the whole way. She did nothing but smile. I sat her down and closed the door and took my swivel chair I'd vacated only such a short time before.

"Jasmine," I said, "what the hell's going on?"

Her grin got bigger. "I don't know what all the fuss is about."

"Me either, so why don't you tell me?"

"Newborn babies get it done every day. What's the big deal?"

"Newborn babies get what done, Jasmine?"

Her grin was just about to pop off her face, and for the first time since I'd known her, she looked downright pretty. "I circumcised him."

I didn't say anything for a minute. I just sat there and crossed my legs tight and sighed. She added, "I think I'm ready for a divorce now, Milt, what do you think?"

It took another hour to get the story out, and by that time the ambulance attendants had managed to get Lester out of the station and over to the hospital. What had happened was basically this: Lester, being none too bright, had forgotten that his wife was on days, so after work—he worked in his daddy's feed store—he went drinking with some of his cronies and ended up bringing some lovely back to his own house.

Now, as I understand it, although Jasmine had known about her husband's philandering, she never actually caught him at it. Well, this night she sure as hell did. She comes home, walks in the bedroom to flip off her shoes, and sees Lester in an unnatural, and very compromising, position with a waitress from the Sidewinder Lounge. Luckily, Jasmine must have forgotten about the service revolver strapped to her hip. Instead, she whacked the waitress in the head a few times with the shoe she'd managed to get off, but the waitress was able to get to her clothes and get the hell out of Dodge.

Meanwhile, old dumb Lester was sitting in the bed saying things like "Honey, it ain't what you think it is." Whereupon Miz Jasmine takes her cuffs off her belt, cuffs her hubby to the bedpost, ties his legs down to the bottom runners with two of his Sunday-go-to-meeting ties, and whacks off his foreskin with a steak knife. Now, Lester being Lester, he didn't take to this right off, squirmed when he shoulda been still, and gets him a nice nick in the old pecker, which started bleeding like a stuck pig, or a stuck pecker, take your pick. Jasmine called the ambulance, but Lester refused to go to the hospital until he'd seen his blushing bride arrested and the key thrown away.

After hearing the story, what could I do but heave a sigh? I said, "Jasmine, that wasn't the brightest thing in the world you coulda done."

"Well, we'd already been talking to the doctor about having that done. He got himself an infection last spring 'cause of that foreskin. His mama shoulda had that taken care of when he was a baby but she didn't. 'Sides, he was gonna use my insurance coverage to have it done! I just saved myself some aggravation."

The really terrible part of it was that Jasmine hadn't stopped grinning through the whole story. Reminded me of something I read one time about some ancient culture where when the soldiers caught their enemy they'd throw 'em to the women. Got so the enemy would rather commit suicide than be taken alive. Can't hardly blame 'em.

Since, with all his screaming, Lester had neglected to sign the complaint form against his wife before the attendants took him to the hospital, I had no real reason to lock Jasmine up. So I just sent her on home instead, knowing Lester would be spending the night at the hospital and would be out of harm's way. After she left, the deputies and I discussed the situation in depth as is our right and duty, and then I took off for home, only a million times tireder than I'd been the first time I took off for home.

But eventful days don't like to pass on lightly. That's probably the only reason I checked the mail on the entry-hall table when I got home the second time. There was a square, heavy-bond envelope sitting there, addressed to me. With the light from my sister's sconce candles on either side of the table, I opened and read my mail.

I suppose there's only so many times you can feel a marriage is over. I felt it when LaDonna left me. And felt it again when I went to the funeral of her uncle and felt like the odd man out. Of course, I also felt it when I got my copy of the divorce papers in the mail. Each time saying to myself, "Well, this is it. The marriage is over. Really over." Standing there with my mail in my hand, I felt like maybe this was the final straw. The straw that would truly break the back of the marriage. An invitation to my wife's wedding. Well, maybe this time it really is over.

The next morning when I came down to breakfast I was not so pleasantly surprised to see Bernblatt sitting at the table with my sister, laughing and talking and eating a bran muffin, and wearing a faded blue T-shirt, this one with the legend, in equally dirty-white lettering, "Vote Republican—It's Easier Than Thinking."

Jewel saw me first and the expression on her face made Bernblatt turn in my direction. "Hi, Deputy," he greeted.

"What the hell are you doing here?"

"Milton!" Jewel said.

"I was thinking about something," Bernblatt said.

I sat down at the table and got the last bran muffin, which was a lot smaller than the one Bernblatt had. "What?" I asked.

"The guy Annette Tapp was shacked up with—"

I made a noise in my throat and nodded my head at Jewel. She just laughed. "God, Milton, I have heard the expression before."

"Just watch what you say in front of my sister," I said, glaring at Bernblatt.

Bernblatt grinned. "I don't know, Deputy. I think your sister may be a lot cooler than you give her credit for."

Jewel blushed and giggled and got up from the table, taking some plates with her. Over her shoulder she said, "That's right, Deputy. I'm cool."

She and Bernblatt looked at each other and grinned. I just glared. At everybody. Anybody. Hell, if the cat'd walked in right then, I'da glared at him too. "So what about the guy she was shacked up with?"

"Who was he?"

"How the hell do I know?"

"Was he, say, um, just for instance, Colombian?"

"Jesus."

"Well?"

"I doubt it."

"Why?"

A little louder than I intended, I said, "Because we don't have any goddamned Colombians in Oklahoma!"

"That a fact?"

"Yeah, that's a goddamn fact!"

"Not one?"

"No! Not even one!"

"Ever?"

"Never!"

"I suppose you have proof of that statement?"

"Go screw yourself in a light socket, Bernblatt. You make me tired."

"So, you got any leads on this cat?"

"Nary a one."

"You got somebody watching the place?"

"What do you think? I'm stupid or something?"

"You want me to answer that?"

I finished my muffin and pushed myself away from the breakfast table. "I gotta go to work. You coming?"

Jewel stuck her head out of the kitchen. "Or you could stay for another cup of coffee."

"You're coming," I said, taking him by the arm and leading him out the door. But not fast enough not to hear Jewel's parting comment.

"See you this evening, Marv. Dinner's at seven."

He grinned at her over his shoulder. "Thanks, Jewel. I'm really looking forward to a home-cooked meal."

"Not at this house," I said under my breath.

NINE

BY THE TIME I GOT to the station, there was a message for me from Mrs. Jacobsen, Lois Bell's mama. The message said she'd be there in two days, coming into the Tulsa airport, and could I have someone there to meet her? Yeah, I figured I could handle that. I called her back, got the name of the airline, the arrival time and gate number, and told her I'd pick her up myself. After I hung up, I dialed another number. Grinning like an idiot, I listened as the phone rang. When a lady answered, I asked to speak to U.S. Marshal Jackson Taylor. It took a minute, but I had him. Boy, did I have him good.

"Marshal Taylor?"

"Yeah, Deputy? What can I do for you?"

"Nothing, Marshal Taylor. Absolutely nothing. Just called to inform you that the bodies of the Bell family will be ready for release on Saturday."

"Well, that's real cooperative of you, Deputy. Thanks for letting me know."

"Course, you may have to fight the next of kin to get 'em. Seems to me Lois Bell's mama might have priority over you."

"What?"

I giggled and hung up. Nobody never said I wasn't in touch with the child within me. Then I put in my second call of the morning, to Dr. Jim.

"Dr. Jim, it's Milt."

"You getting me in more trouble with the feds, Milton?"

"Oh, just a little."

"Thanks heaps and bunches."

"I was just wondering if Marshal Taylor ever showed up with that court order?"

"Nope, he never did."

"Well, look for him. He's probably on his way over now. If you can, I'd like you to lose those bodies until Saturday."

"Lose the bodies. Milton, them's the only bodies in the morgue right now! How in the hell am I supposed to lose 'em? And why Saturday?"

"Like you told me before, you're the doctor. Losing 'em's your job. It's just that Saturday Lois Bell's mama's gonna come identify them."

"Well, no shit! You finally found the next of kin! I'll be goddamned. Didn't know you had it in you!"

"Thanks for the vote of confidence. Anyway, Taylor's gonna be chomping at the bit now. And we're too close. Lose them bodies."

"What bodies?" he said, and hung up.

I pressed down the thingamabob on the phone and redialed. This call I knew wouldn't be near as much fun as the previous two had been. After two rings, my lady's voice said, "Hello?"

"Hi, honey." Dead silence greeted me. "Baby, listen, I'm real sorry about last night." Still no response. "Glenda Sue, you there?"

"Milton, you're more trouble than you're worth."

"Honey, I said I'm sorry. And I mean it. I really am. It's this damned job."

"You know, sometimes," she said, "I think you think more about Lois Bell than you do about me."

"Glenda Sue . . ."

She sighed. "See you Friday, tiger," she said, and hung up. Tiger, that was a good sign. A real good sign. Well, things were finally beginning to look up. I had Jackson Taylor on the run and my sex life was on the upswing. Of course, I still didn't know who'd killed Lois Bell, but other than that little bitty old thing. . . . I still wondered, though, no matter what Bernblatt thought, if maybe everything was really just as it seemed. Lois Bell committed suicide and accidentally gassed her entire family, although I did keep wondering about the bump on her head, and I still wanted to know what Neville Crouch had been doing near Lois's house.

At two-thirty I decided to take a little trip over to the elementary school. I parked in the parking lot, right behind Crouch's Karmann Ghia. I rolled my window down because the cold snap had left, leaving high humidity and unusual heat for the time of year. When the bell rang, I listened as the kids piled out of the building, shouting and stomping and ready for their freedom.

At a little after three, the teachers started their escape. At three-fifteen, I saw Crouch come through a side door, heading for his car. He was deep in conversation with another teacher, and he was almost on me before he saw my car sitting there blocking his. I got out as the other teacher waved good-bye and walked on to her car.

"Hey, Mr. Crouch," I said, all smiles.

He wasn't returning my smile. I tried not to feel slighted. "What are you doing here?"

"Just thought we might jaw a minute."

"I've had a long day, Deputy. I want to go home. If you'll excuse me...."

He headed for the driver's side of the Ghia and opened the door, throwing his book bag onto the passenger seat.

I walked over and shut the door before he slid in. "How 'bout I buy you a nice cold iced tea?"

"Why don't you just tell me what the hell you want with me? Okay? Can you do me that little favor?" His voice was getting loud and other teachers coming out of the building were looking at him.

I ushered him into the passenger side of my squad car and got into the driver's side. We drove in silence to Bernie's Chat and Chew, which was only a few blocks from the school. We silently entered the café. Finding a booth in the corner, I sat us down and ordered two iced teas. The teenage waitress wasn't impressed with our order, but went off to get it nonetheless.

"Unusually hot for this time of year, don't you think?" I asked, as she set down the teas.

"Cut the bullshit," Crouch said after she'd left. "What is it you want?"

I heaved an aggrieved sigh. "Well, I'll tell you, Neville. Can I call you Neville?"

"No."

I laughed. "I'll tell you. It's just that I'd truly like to know what you were doing over by Miz Bell's house the other day. I'd truly like to know that."

"I already told you."

"Yeah. Did you know there's a statute still on the books in Oklahoma that using profanity against an officer of the law is a criminal offense? I believe what you told me was it wasn't none of my, excuse the expression, 'fucking' business. Isn't that what you said?"

He laughed and leaned back against the cracked Naugahyde booth. "You wanna arrest me for using the word 'fuck' in your presence, Deputy, you go right ahead."

I laughed, too. "Now, I never said I was gonna arrest you. I only said I could."

"Moot point."

"Ain't it just? Anyway, what were you doing by Miz Bell's house?"

His face was turning red and he shook his head a few times. "Why?" he asked, exasperated as all get-out. "Why? Just tell me why you need to know! Okay?"

"Because Miz Bell was having an affair with somebody and I think that somebody mighta killed her and her whole family. I just wanted to know if that somebody was you."

Crouch's red complexion faded until he looked like somebody'd dipped him in flour. "Jesus. Come on, Milt! My God!"

"You wanna tell me what you were doing over by her house the other day?"

He was still for so long I thought maybe the shock had put him in a coma, but finally he leaned forward, all conspiratorial-like, and said, in a harsh whisper, "Look, I was seeing a lady. On Grapevine Road. But it wasn't Lois Bell! I swear to God! I barely knew her!"

"Who were you seeing?"

He fell back against the cushion of the booth again, his color still a floury white. "I can't tell you that."

"Well, I think maybe you'd better. Less you want your ass thrown in jail."

Leaning forward again, he said, "I can't! Look, man, she's married! This will ruin her. Can't you understand that?"

I leaned forward, too. "Can't you understand that unless I have the cooperation of this supposed married lady, I can't believe a word you're telling me?"

"I swear it's the truth!"

I leaned back and threw up my hands. "Well, that makes all the goddamn difference in the world!"

"You swear you won't tell anyone else? You swear this will stay with just you and me?"

"And her. I gotta talk to her."

"Shit. Oh, shit." A man defeated is not a pretty sight. And I can't say I was right proud of myself or my profession. "Shirley Milkin."

"Man, you are a fool" is all I said, as I got up and paid the bill and headed back to my squad car. I figured anybody fool enough to mess with Bubba Milkin's wife was fool enough to walk back to the school.

I knew Bubba worked at the refinery on the Tulsa highway and his shift wouldn't be over till past six, plus then he'd have to drive home. I had time enough to confirm Neville Crouch's story. I figured Shirley'd be ready for me because Crouch would have been on the phone in the café to her before the door shut good behind me.

Bubba Milkin woulda made it to all-pro fullback if he hadn't landed in jail. He'd been in his second year at OU, giving the competition a lotta shit and some broken bones along the way, when he had his little trouble. He'd gone off campus with some fellas and gotten a little loaded at a bar and proceeded to kick some ass. One guy died of his injuries and two were hospitalized for a goodly while. And Bubba ended up serving a three-year sentence for manslaughter.

After he got out, he came home and married his high school sweetheart, Shirley Dobie. Of course, the fact that she was already married when he got out didn't seem to mean much to old Bubba. No one ever knew exactly what had happened to Shirley Dobie's first husband. I guess nobody really wanted to know. Why in the hell anybody would mess with Shirley Milkin now, why any fool would do it, I just didn't know. But I was gonna tread careful. I didn't want Neville Crouch's death on my conscience.

Shirley was waiting at the screen door when I got there. A little spit of a girl, no bigger than a minute, with bright, carrot-red hair and freckles big as dimes all over her. Her hands were shaking against the screen door as she stood there. "He was here," she whispered. "Okay. That what you need to know?"

"Let me in, Shirley. You can just tell Bubba I was here asking if you seen anything funny at the Bell house back when it happened."

"I didn't see nothin'."

"I'm not really asking you that, Shirley. That's just what you're supposed to tell Bubba. In case anybody says anything to him about seeing my car." I couldn't help but wonder how in the hell she'd managed to pull off an affair for however long it had lasted.

"Oh," she said, and opened the door. I went in and sat down on the couch next to her.

"Shirley, you wanna tell me about you and Neville Crouch?"

"No."

"Has he been coming over here, Shirley?"

"Yes."

"For how long?"

She shrugged. "I dunno. Awhile."

"A month? A week? A year?"

She shrugged. "Couple weeks."

"Okay, Shirley, thank you." I got up and left, hoping the little thing could pull it off.

I went back to the station and spent the rest of my day worrying about what was coming that evening. Tonight was the night the county commissioners met. And tonight was the night me and Billy Moulini was gonna give 'em some shit. The thought that these people were my ultimate employers, me being a county employee and all, did enter my mind from time to time that day, like maybe every other minute. But, I figured, just because I was a county em-

ployee didn't mean I had no right to my own
personal grievances. Right? Damned straight!

But, of course, standing between me and Billy and
the county commissioners was dinner. Dinner with
Bernblatt. The thought of just not showing up never
entered my head. I wasn't about to leave Bernblatt
alone with my sister. Or vice versa. I just wasn't sure
who'd be in the biggest trouble.

I got home to my mountain about six o'clock that
evening, which gave me an hour to work on my sister's guilt before Bernblatt showed up. I mean, what
did she need an obnoxious asshole like Bernblatt for
when she had a perfectly good married former boy-
friend braying at her heels? Huh? Of course, if Jewel
remained true to form, her dinner alone could turn
the lecherous newshound off completely.

I walked into the kitchen and sniffed. So far so
good. Because of company, Jewel Anne was pulling
out all the stops. And if there's one thing I've noticed about Jewel's cooking, it gets worse the fancier she tries. Tonight she was attempting Stroganoff.
I knew that only from the open cookbook lying by
the stove, its corners beginning to singe from the
nearness of the heating oil. The lady herself was
standing by the sink peeling carrots.

"Hey, Jewel," I greeted.

"Oh, hi, Milton," she said, barely turning around.

"What's for dinner?" I asked, barely able to sup-
press a giggle.

"Stroganoff with parslied noodles, candied carrots, and Waldorf salad."

"You know, that was real nice of you inviting Bernblatt over for dinner, but you didn't have to do that."

She glanced around at me. "I know I didn't have to, Milton. I wanted to."

"Why?"

She shrugged and turned back to the sink. "He makes me laugh."

Oh, shit, I thought. Anything but that. I turned and walked to the living room and flopped down in my easy chair figuring there was no amount of guilt in the world that could compete with him making her laugh. I'd barely picked up the evening paper when Jewel Anne stuck her head in the living-room doorway.

"Milton, run upstairs and bring down some of your beer, will you? I'm sure Marv would like one." Her head popped back before I could throw anything at it.

Dinner, as usual, was a disaster. The cubes of meat in the Stroganoff were alternately burned or raw, the noodles were *al dente* like a son of a bitch, the carrots were soggy, and the Waldorf salad was runny.

Halfway through, with his mouth full of food, Bernblatt said, "Jewel, this is delicious."

I shoulda known. Anybody as skinny as Bernblatt surely had no appreciation of food. I sat through dinner like the odd man out. The kids loved Bernblatt. Jewel loved Bernblatt. Bernblatt loved the kids. And he obviously had the hots for my sister. Yeah, I was the odd man out, all right. At that point, I didn't love a goddamn soul. Then the phone rang. I got up to answer it.

"Hello?"

"Ah, hi, Milt. This is Harmon."

I grinned real big and said real loud, "Oh, hi, Harmon."

"Is Jewel Anne around?"

"Why, yes, she is, Harmon. She surely is around. Hold on just a minute." Covering the mouthpiece with the heel of my hand, I called into the dining room. "Oh, Jewel! Phone call. It's Harmon."

I'd heard her chair scraping back while I was still talking to Harmon on the phone, and before I got out the whole announcement, Jewel had grabbed the handset. Course, that didn't stop me from completing my sentence. I went back to the table and answered at great length all the questions the children had about who Harmon was. Bernblatt just sat there sullenly, trying to chew his food.

At seven-thirty I excused myself to make it to the county commissioners' meeting by eight o'clock. Nobody seemed to notice me leaving.

The county commissioners met every other Thursday in a room at the new recreation center. I've never been sure why they call it the new recreation center, but they always do. It was built in 1954 and there'd never been another recreation center, but to this day it's called the "new recreation center." What it is is a big building next to the community pool with a gym for basketball, a library, and meeting rooms. Since the county built it, the commissioners are the only ones who don't have to pay to have a meeting there.

That Thursday night there was the usual crowd: all six commissioners, five middle-age white guys with their own businesses and one middle-age white woman, who'd inherited the position when her husband had a stroke the year before. Gladys was there of course, because part of her duties as sheriff's clerk was clerking every other week at the commission meetings. The audience, if it could be called that, consisted of me and Billy Moulini; Johnnie Rainwater, the representative of the part of the Indian reservation that touched on Prophesy County, who was always in attendance just in case; Mrs. Marilou Pepper, who brought her knitting to the meetings every other week; and three ominous-looking men in business suits.

I followed Billy to the front row where we took our seats. Some of the commissioners saw him, of course, but instead of greeting him like a long-lost brother, they just whispered among themselves.

The meeting was called to order and there was an hour-long discussion on whether to consider discussing at a later date the need for expansion of the sewerage system. A vote was taken and it was decided that expansion of the sewerage system would be discussed at a meeting in the spring. Then, as usual, a motion was brought by one of the commissioners that they get paid. This was discussed for another hour and was, as usual, tabled.

They went on to discuss discussing issues such as a bond election for a new highway to be built through property Commissioner Perkins had recently acquired; declaring a county-wide holiday on February 11, which was somewhere around the time somebody thought Prophesy County may have been established, back in 1842; and various and sundry other motions that were boring as watching dog shit harden.

At midnight, the mike was opened to discussion. That's when my friend Billy stood up and walked to the podium.

"Everybody knows me," he started. "But anyway, my name's Bill Moulini and I own some property here in Prophesy County. Property that's currently being threatened."

There were some sniggers by some of the commissioners and one of them said, "Who's threatening you, Billy?"

Billy turned and, with a gesture that has won many an Academy Award, pointed at the three business suits. "These gentlemen here, Oscar. They're threatening to turn my property into time-share condos for a bunch of rich Texans.''

Now, I gotta hand it to old Billy. There's nothing like the threat of a Texan to make an Oklahoma county commissioner sit up and take notice. But Oscar Lobach, the head commissioner, said, ''Now, Billy, them condos gonna bring a lot of money into the county.''

''Oh, yeah? How's that? They're buying the land dirt cheap, getting a break on the taxes, no doubt, and water hookups and electric, gonna sell them condos for a fat, juicy profit, then they're gonna sit empty nine months outta the year. The other three months, all you're gonna have is a bunch of BMWs zipping up and down the mountain. They ain't gonna buy their food here, we ain't got no health food stores; they ain't gonna buy their clothes here, we ain't got no Gucci outlet. How in the hell, Oscar, you think this is gonna bring money into the county? Unless, of course, these boys are greasing your pockets a little.''

''Now just hold on a goddamn minute, Billy Moulini—''

''I got the mike here, Oscar. Now you fellas listen to me. I got my lawyers on this and they got an injunction stopping these people from building. Now when that injunction runs out, I'm just gonna get me another. I can tie this up in court till hell freezes over, boys, you know I can. So why don't we just quit screwing around and tell these Texans to go on back where they come from?''

Oscar Lobach was looking a fair shade of unhealthy as he asked, "You through, Billy?"

"Not by a long shot, Oscar." And with a dramatic flourish, he left the podium and returned to his seat next to me.

That's when one of the suits got up and walked to the podium. "Gentlemen," he started, then, nodding his head toward Billy, "and Mr. Moulini," which got a laugh out of the commissioners, "my name's Arnold Task and I represent the Metropolis Developing Corporation. What Mr. Moulini here just stated couldn't be farther from the truth. We've gotten no incentive on taxes, water, or electric hookups to build in this area. The reason, the only reason, we want to build on Mountain Falls Road is the same reason I'm sure Mr. Moulini built there in the first place. Because it's beautiful—"

"Won't be long after you assholes move in!" Billy interrupted. Mrs. Pepper giggled around her knitting.

"We have no intention," Task continued, "of disturbing the natural beauty of the area. That, the natural beauty, will be our main selling point to those people interested in the condos in the first place. Whyever would we want to spoil that?''

Heckling again, Billy said, "'Cause that's the only thing you know how to do!''

"Billy!" Oscar yelled from the commissioner's table. "Don't you be interrupting any more. You hear me?"

"The dead hear you, Oscar!"

"Gentlemen, Mr. Moulini's assertion that the buyers of the condos won't be using Prophesy County merchants is dead wrong. In studies we've done of our other projects all over the state, we've found that—"

And then the numbers started. So-and-so percent of such-and-such and on and on and on. And the commissioners were eating it up. One commissioner owned a heavy equipment rental company, which would be utilized in the construction, another owned a trucking company, a third a concrete mixing plant, and so on and so on. For any of them to vote no on the condo time-share project would mean throwing money out of their own pockets. I've never yet met a commissioner willing to do that. Billy and I were whupped, only he didn't know it.

As we walked out the door together, he said, "Don't you worry none, Milt. I bought the Munksy farm today and I been talking to old Haywood. I think I can make him an offer. With that and my lawyers working on it, they ain't gonna win."

I just nodded my head, depressed as all get-out, and wondering how much of this money old Billy was putting down he considered my share. As I barely had a pot to piss in, I was beginning to feel like maybe I just sold my soul to the devil. A pudgy, cigar-smoking devil.

"Let me buy you a drink," Billy announced, taking my arm and escorting me to his Lincoln parked in the handicapped parking. Knowing which side of the bread the butter's on, I didn't think it politic to give him a ticket, though that is one thing that chaps my ass like a son of a bitch. People parking in handicapped parking who aren't. Handicapped, I mean.

Anyway, he led me to his Lincoln and we both got in, me in the passenger's seat. I started to reach for my seat belt, thinking we must be going to the Sidewinder for a drink, when old Billy opened a leather-covered built-in box between his seat and mine and I discovered Billy's bar. The hinged lid swung up and had two rows of fancy bar glasses. The underpart was filled with pint bottles of liquor. Another violation if ever there was one. I figured if I hung around Billy Moulini for long, I'd compromise myself to death.

"What's your poison?" he asked.

Looking over the lid, I spied me some Jack Daniels, which I indicated to Billy would do me just fine. We sat there for a minute, both sipping our whiskeys.

"Lord, I wanna win this," Billy finally said.

"Yes, sir, me, too."

"What that asshole lawyer said wasn't true. About why I built on the mountain."

"Oh? Why was it, then?" I asked, sipping and grinning.

Billy leaned his silver head against the Lincoln's plush headrest. "'Cause of my daddy." He took a long pull on his drink and glanced over at me.

"You're too young to have known my daddy, I suppose."

"Yeah, I guess so."

Billy laughed a faraway laugh. "God, what a rounder! Wheeler-dealer deluxe. Guess that's where I got it from. 'Cept Daddy never made much. Shit, boy, we barely had two pennies to scrape together when I was a kid. But anyway, about the mountain. We'd go hunting up there, me and my daddy. I had me a shotgun bigger than me by the time I was six years old. Kilt my first rabbit when I was seven. Bagged my first deer when I was eight. Took every ounce a' muscle I had just to lift the goddamn gun!" He laughed, far away in his memories. "Everything I know, every dirty story, every moral, every move on a woman, every deal that can be made, I learned from Daddy while we were up on that mountain. He died when I was fifteen. Kilt in a knife fight over a fishy deck of cards. I still got them cards." He opened his glove compartment and brought out an aged deck of Bicycle Cards. I rifled through them. "They're a marked deck all right. But you'd never know it just looking."

I tried to see the markings, but in the dim light from the streetlight, I couldn't see a blamed thing.

Billy took the deck back, rifled them through his fingers, then put them back in the glove compartment. "Anyway," he said, "that's why I built on the mountain. And that's why no bastard's taking it away from me. See you soon, boy."

Having been dismissed, I handed him my glass, which still had about half a finger of Jack Daniels in it. As I got out of the car, I saw him swallow the contents and place the glass back in the bar. I went on to my '55.

Although it was getting on to one o'clock in the morning, I didn't feel like driving home. I also knew better than driving by Glenda Sue's at this time of night. Instead, I found myself wandering the streets of Longbranch, enjoying the dead calm of the town in the early morning. Just me and a few stray dogs on the street, that was all. At some point I ended up at the Bell place, don't ask me why. And it took me a minute to realize there was a light on in the house. A light that shouldn't have been on.

I turned off the interior light of my car before opening the door and left the door open a crack to keep from making a sound. I still had the key to the house in my pocket, although I really didn't need it. The front door was again ajar. Entering the house, I heard a sound, like a sob, coming from the back. Slowly, I traced my steps through the filth of the living room to the hall, quietly moving toward the back. It was at about that point I thought of drawing my gun. Since it was only like the third time I'd ever done it for real, it's not exactly an instant reflex.

Anyway, I had the gun in my hand, afraid to take off the safety because of the clicking noise it makes. The house was so damned quiet I knew that click would be as loud as a fart in church. I entered the master bedroom at a crouch, my gun pointing toward the bed. "Sheriff's department, hold it right there," I said.

Junior Dickey jumped up from where he'd been lying on the bed, suppressed a sob, and headed for the window. Luckily, he tripped in the mess of laundry on the floor.

For want of anything better to do, I went over and sat on him. He was crying and squirming fit to beat the band. "Hold on now, Junior. Just calm down. I'm not gonna hurt you. Calm down, now." I gradually let up the pressure as he gradually calmed down. Finally I sat down next to him on the floor and holstered my gun. "You wanna tell me what you're doing here?" I asked.

He didn't answer, unless you consider bursting into tears an answer. I patted him on the back for a time until the tears finally subsided. "Junior, we need to talk."

He hiccuped.

"I need to know what you're doing here."

He shook his head.

"Junior, if I ask you a question, will you just shake your head yes or no?"

He shook his head yes.

"You been keeping company with Miz Bell over at Lake Blue?"

Again, he burst into tears and I patted him on the back.

"Junior, I'm gonna take that as a yes."

He slowly, agonizingly, nodded his head in the affirmative.

Again I patted his back. "I'm real sorry, boy. I know this is rough on you."

Again the nod of the head.

"I gotta ask you a question. You know anything about her death you haven't told me?"

To my surprise, he nodded his head.

"What?"

There was a sob and then he looked up at me, his eyes red and swollen. "She didn't do it" was all he said.

"Why's that?"

"'Cause!" he screamed. "She wouldn't! She just wouldn't!"

"I know it's hard to believe . . ."

He hit me in the shoulder with his fist. It didn't hurt, just surprised me. "No! She wouldn't! She loved me! We were happy!"

"That was at Lake Blue, son. Here . . . well . . ."

"She was going to divorce him."

"Boy, sometimes that's easier said than done."

In a far-off, dreamy voice he said, "We were gonna take the kids and buy a house down in Houston. She was gonna get a job in a bank while I went to school. We were gonna buy a piano. A baby grand. She played the piano real well. We'd read the kids bedtime stories before they went to sleep, each in their own little bed, then we'd go into the living room and she'd play for me while I studied. And then we'd go to bed. And we'd make love every night."

He stopped and sobbed and leaned against me, his arms going round my neck. I held him and let him cry. Thanks to circumstances and the Witness Protection Program, Lois Bell was already living a fantasy life. It was just that the fantasy she was living was nasty and mean. Why not make a pretty one? And populate it with a pretty, young boy who idolized her, dress up her kids in Little Lord Fauntleroy and Mary Janes, and live in a pretty blue-and-peach house in Houston? Sipping brandy and playing the baby grand? Reading each other sweet poetry and making love every night? Junior and Alexandra Kincade Dickey. Bad as the boy was hurting, *my* heart was bleeding for Lois Bell.

After he finally calmed down, I took him out of the house and out to my car. I felt I'd have a better time of talking to him away from that awful house.

A thought had occurred to me and I felt I had to go with it. Distasteful as it was. "Junior, you and Lois had all these plans. What happened to them?"

He looked at me like I was crazy. "She died, Mr. Kovak."

I nodded my head. "Yes, son, I know that. But before she died . . ."

"We were gonna do it. Come January. She was gonna get Bill drunk, which he did every night anyway, and then when he passed out, she was gonna get the kids and slip them out their bedroom window and we were gonna drive to Houston."

"Just like that?"

"Huh?"

"That was your big plan?"

"It woulda worked!"

I nodded my head. Then I asked, "Just supposing, what would you have done if Lois decided at the last minute she couldn't do it?"

"Huh?"

"Woulda made you real mad, wouldn't it, Junior?"

"Huh?"

"Mad enough, maybe, to want to make it all go away?"

"Oh, Jesus! Oh, shit! Mr. Kovak, you don't think I—" Then he burst into tears again. "I didn't!" He sobbed. "I wouldn't hurt her for anything! I'd gouge out my eyes before I'd hurt a hair on her head!"

"Okay, son, okay. One more question: Was that you in here the other day that ran off?"

Sheepishly he nodded his head. "Yes, sir."

"What were you doing in the house?"

He sighed. "I'd gone over to the apartment on Lake Blue to make sure there was nothing there, you know... anyway, I knew the receipts for the apartment were around there someplace, but I couldn't find them. I came over here to see..."

I nodded. "Yeah, they were here."

"Oh, that's how you know about the place at Lake Blue?"

"Yeah."

He looked thoughtful for a moment. "Why would she have 'em here, though?"

I looked at him. The kid had a point. Why in the hell would a lady bring home evidence that she was shacking up with somebody else? Didn't make a whole lot of sense. But frankly, I was just too damned tired to think about it. Me and Scarlett, I'd think about that tomorrow.

TEN

I DROVE ON HOME and as I pulled into my parking spot by the corral, I immediately got mad as shit. Because I was parking behind Bernblatt's rental. And not only that, every light in the house was out! And this from a woman who complained that me spending the night out with my lady friend was a bad influence on her children! Did I bring Glenda Sue home? I did not! Did I bring strange women I barely knew into my upstairs bedroom? I did not!

I sat in the car for about five minutes, counting to ten about fifty times. That's what my daddy taught me. "When they really get to you, Milton, just count to ten. As many times as it takes. Because there's nothing lower in this world than a man who'll hit a woman. And there's nothing a woman likes better than for you to get really pissed and yell at her. Gives her ammunition." Course, all that advice had to do with courting young ladies, not dealing with his own darling daughter. But when you find something that works, you stick with it.

Finally I was calm enough to go inside. I unlocked the door (she'd had the presence of mind to lock up before retiring to her love nest, I'll give her that) and went straight up to my room.

The next morning I'll be damned if the bastard wasn't sitting at the kitchen table, the kids surrounding him, eating breakfast in blue jeans and a Grateful Dead T-shirt like he owned the damned place. I took Jewel's chair, as she was at the stove cooking, and waited to be served.

"Good morning, Deputy," Bernblatt said.

I took a sip of juice. "Good morning."

Bernblatt grinned. "Sleep well?"

I didn't answer. Jewel set a plate of runny scrambled eggs in front of me. "You got in awfully late, didn't you?" she asked. Accusing me! Accusing *me* of God only knows what!

I was saved from answering by the blast of the school bus horn. Carl got up and grabbed his books, kissed his mother good-bye, and said good-bye to Bernblatt. As an afterthought, he said good-bye to me.

"Guess we'd better be hitting the road," Leonard said. "Ready, Marlene?"

"Sure. Bye, Marv," she said, and kissed him on the cheek. I was getting mad. Really, really mad. Who the hell did this guy think he was?

The kids took off and I sat there staring at the scrambled eggs. Bernblatt got up. "I gotta go, Jewel. Thanks for everything." He waved good-bye to me and, pulling his jacket off the back of the chair, left.

"Well, you're sure quiet this morning," Jewel said, taking a chair across from me and sipping from her steaming coffee cup. A steaming coffee cup full of the weakest, puniest coffee you ever drank in your life. Looks like tea!

"Woman, you got some gall," I finally managed to say.

"I beg your pardon?"

"Gall. The Jewish people call it chutzpah. Uncouth slobs like me sometimes refer to it as balls. As in big, shiny brass ones."

"Would you like to spell this out, Milton? Because I haven't got the faintest idea what you're talking about."

I leaned forward in my chair, feeling the veins popping in my neck and my face going red. But, people, I was mad. Seriously mad. "I'm talking about you sleeping with that goddamn Yankee asshole!"

"Oh." Jewel sipped her coffee like it was tasty.

"Oh? Oh! That's all you can say is 'Oh'?"

"You're referring to my night of unbridled passion with Marv?"

I leaned back in my chair, shaking my head. "You admit it. You act like you're proud of it! I'm just glad Mama's not alive to see this...."

I stopped because of her laughter. It's hard to get into a real self-righteous indignation when somebody's laughing at you.

"What the hell are you laughing at, woman?"

She stopped laughing, took another sip of her coffee, sighed long and hard, then pointed one long, piano player's finger at me. "Don't call me 'woman' in that particular tone of voice ever again. And don't ever say that about Mama again. And, also, don't go around accusing people of things you don't know a damned thing about!"

I just glared at her while she glared back at me. "If it's any of your damned business, when I decide to go to bed with anybody, and it could very well be Marv Bernblatt, I'll do it away from my home. I will not bring that into my children's home. For your information, although it is *none* of your damned business, Marv had a few too many beers last night and I asked him to stay over rather than drive all the way back to the Longbranch Inn. He slept in Leonard's room over the garage. Leonard stayed with Carl. Now, are you satisfied?"

Not one to let go of an issue with a smidgen of grace, I said, "So it's okay for him to get stinking drunk in front of the kids, but I can't have one goddamn beer in my own goddamn living room?"

Jewel threw up her hands, stood up and walked to her bedroom, and slammed the door behind her. I left for the station house.

I barely got sat down in my chair good when Gladys stuck her head in the door. "Milton...."

"No visitors!"

"Your sister."

I stood up as Jewel walked in. "Hi," I said sweetly.

"I need you to take me someplace."

"Oh? Your car break down again?"

She thought about it for a minute then said, "Yes." That may have been the first lie she'd ever told in her life. And she was real bad at it.

"Where do you need me to take you?"

"To the hospital."

I came around from my side of the desk fast. "Jewel, you sick?"

"No."

I took hold of her arm gently. "One of the kids?"

"No."

I let go of her arm. "Then what is it?"

She looked down at her toes, sighed, then looked up at me. "We have an appointment."

"We?"

"Yes."

"With who?"

"Whom."

"Jewel Anne."

"Dr. Marston."

I went back around to my swivel chair and sank into it. "Ain't no goddamn way."

Jewel turned, walked just outside my door, and said, very loudly, "Oh, Sheriff, you got a minute?"

I jumped up and ran to where she stood. "That's blackmail."

"You bet your shiny heinie." She smiled sweetly. I got my suit coat and led her out to my '55.

I don't like going to the Longbranch Memorial Hospital. That's where Mama died. That's where I had my hemorrhoidectomy twelve years ago. That's where my favorite of my ex-wife's uncles died only a couple of years ago. That's where Dr. Jim's morgue was. I didn't like the place. I didn't like going in the place. I didn't like driving by the place. But let's get one thing straight: I have nothing against shrinks. Really. They have their place in a polite society. They make real good dinnertable conversation. Their names look good on boards of directors of charitable organizations. But their place definitely wasn't inside the head of one Milton Louis Kovak.

I parked the car in the parking area reserved for people going to the hospital annex, which was an ugly wing tacked on to the back of the hospital proper and covered in a completely different color and style of brick from the original building. Jewel Anne immediately got out of the car and hobbled toward the entrance. For want of anything more stimulating to do, I followed. She led me past the main receptionist, down a hall to a door marked "Counseling," so that everybody and their brother would know exactly what you were doing, and into the waiting room. The room was decorated in plastic. Plastic chairs, a plastic couch, wood-grained plastic coffee table, and plastic-covered copies of *People* magazine. And, of course, the receptionist was somebody I knew. Somebody from the church.

We sat down, me on the couch and Jewel as far away as possible in one of the plastic chairs. And we waited. Finally the door next to the receptionist's window opened and the patient before us stepped out. Jasmine Bodine. Why the hell not? Why not let everybody in the goddamn state know Milton Kovak was off his rocker?

"Well, hey, Milt!" Jasmine greeted. "What are you doing here?"

I stood up and shook hands with my deputy. "Just drove my sister over for an appointment," I said, pointedly not looking at said sister. "How's it going?"

Jasmine smiled real big. Pretty smile. "Just great!"

"I noticed Lester hasn't come by to press charges," I said by way of conversation.

The smile never left her face. "No. I went by to see him in the hospital and let him know if he pressed charges I'd eventually get out and find him wherever he was hiding and whack off the rest of his dick."

"Oh."

"So he decided to let it drop. And I get the house and the good car."

"That's nice."

"And the dog."

"That's good."

"And half of everything he makes for the rest of his frigging life."

"Well."

She waved at Jewel. "See ya later," she said to me, and walked out.

I sat back down just in time to bob up again as the door opened and Dr. Marston came out. She led us through the door back into the inner sanctum of nut city. We went down a short hall and ended up in her office, which was a little homier than the waiting room. The couches and chairs were covered in actual, real-life fabric, and there was even a picture on a wall. I looked around the room as if I was interested, all the while wondering how a woman no bigger than a minute was gonna solve my problems. There's something a little bit intimidating about going to an authority figure who's not only smaller than you, more in touch with her female side than you, but younger to boot.

All the while I was contemplating this, Jewel Anne was talking a mile a minute. Most of which I didn't catch. Then Dr. Marston turned to me.

"How do you feel about what Jewel's just said, Mr. Kovak?"

I pulled my attention toward the teacher—sorry, the doctor—and said, "Huh?"

"How do you feel about what your sister just said?"

I shrugged.

"Jewel, how do you feel about Milton's uncommunicative manner?"

"I'm used to it. If he's not screaming swear words or swilling beer, he just sits there like a lump."

This I heard. "Now wait just a goddamn minute!"

"Milton, before we start," Dr. Marston said, "would you mind removing your gun and badge and letting me put them away for you?"

"Huh?"

She stood up and walked toward me, hand outstretched. "Removing your gun and badge will lessen your authoritarian image and increase equity in therapy."

I stood up, removed the gun from my holster, slid the clip out of the butt and into my pocket, and handed her the gun and the little leather case that housed my badge. I felt like I'd been stripped naked for all the world to see.

She walked to her desk, opened the bottom drawer, and placed my gun and badge inside. I watched with a sinking heart as the drawer slowly closed. Dr. Marston sat down again and smiled at me. "Now," she said, "you were saying?"

"What?"

"In response to your sister's comment."

"Ah . . . what was the comment?"

"She said, 'If he's not screaming swear words or swilling beer, he just sits there like a lump.' Your response was, I believe, 'Now wait just a goddamn minute.'"

"Yeah, okay." I sat there a minute trying to get back the good, old self-righteous anger I'd had a minute earlier. Looking over at my sister, who sat there with her own self-righteous look on her face, brought back the feelings in a flash. "I'm getting a little sick and tired of everything being my fault! Like everything in the whole world revolves around me swearing or drinking beer! I don't swear that damned much and I only have a couple of beers after work! And this I have to do in my goddamn bedroom! And then *she* invites company over and let's 'em get drunk on *my* beer!"

"Jewel?"

"See? Did you hear him? *This* is what I have to put up with!"

"My heart bleeds," I muttered.

"Thank you very much," Jewel said, "but your sarcasm is not needed at the moment."

"What was *that* if it wasn't sarcasm? Huh?"

"May I ask a question?" Dr. Marston said.

Jewel Anne and I both shrugged.

"Is this the form your communication usually follows?"

Jewel and I looked at each other then back to the doctor.

"What I'm asking is this: Do you two always go on at each other like this?"

Being the male head of household, I answered. "Yep."

"That's not true," Jewel broke in. "We only go on this way when we're actually talking. You know, in the same room. Most of the time, he's upstairs swilling beer—"

"Goddamn it!"

"Well, it's true!"

"Most of the time I'm upstairs because I know you can't follow me up there and nag!"

"Sure, take advantage of my handicap!"

"It's the only goddamned advantage I can get!"

"Stop!" We both turned to look at Dr. Marston. "This is nonproductive."

"Tell me about it," I muttered under my breath.

"Why did you agree to come here, Milton?" Dr. Marston asked.

"I didn't. She blackmailed me into it."

"So, you have no desire to improve your present home situation?"

"Oh, sure, lay it all on my back!"

"Milton, how do you feel about your present home situation?"

I shrugged.

"Milton, how do you feel about things at home as they now stand?"

I shrugged. Finally, after a lengthy silence, I said, "I feel out of control."

"As if you have no control over the situation?"

"Yeah. What you said."

"Tell me about it."

I shrugged. "It's my house. I pay the house note, the water and electric and telephone bills—"

"Here we go again!" Jewel said.

"Jewel, Milton's talking. Please don't interrupt. You'll get your chance."

I leaned forward. "She doesn't appreciate it at all! I moved her and her kids and her goddamn baby grand all the way from Houston—"

"I paid the moving expenses!"

"Jewel."

"And now I feel like the house isn't mine anymore. It's hers. I have no say-so whatsoever in anything. I can't even sit in the living room without her telling me I'm doing it wrong! I love the kids. They're great. But because of the way she treats me, they're beginning to think of me as just a stick of furniture. I'm mad all the damned time. And so is she! Dr. Marston, I don't want her and the kids to move, but I'm beginning to wonder how else in the world this can be solved."

At that Jewel Anne stood up. "That's quite all right, Milton. The kids and I will be out of your hair by the time you get home from work." She headed for the door. I jumped up and roughly pulled her back to her chair and pushed her down into it.

"Milton," Dr. Marston said.

I held up a hand to stop whatever she'd planned on saying. "Don't do that again! Don't run away from this! You're the one wanted to come to a goddamn shrink! Well, by God, we're here! And you're by God staying!"

"Milton has a point, Jewel. But, Milton, please, no more physical outbursts."

We went on like this for awhile, with nothing exactly new coming out of it all. When Dr. Marston indicated that our time was up, she said, "We have a lot of work to do. Do the two of you agree on that?"

Jewel nodded and I shrugged. "Milton?"

"Yeah, I agree."

"Then I suggest we set some appointments. This isn't like going to your family physician and getting a pill. We have no magic pills here. This is going to take some time."

"How much time?" I asked.

"At this point, I can't tell you. We're probably looking at several months. I'd like to see the two of you at least once a week."

"And who's paying for all this?" I asked. Crude, but it had to be said.

Jewel sighed. "I'll cash in one of my CDs and give it to Dr. Marston. When we've used up all that, then it's your turn. Is that fair?"

I nodded. Dr. Marston stood up and Jewel and I followed. She got my gun and badge from the drawer and handed them to me, holding the .45 casually, and handing it to me butt first like you're supposed to. Most women I knew pick up a gun like it's a dead rat. Made me wonder a little about the good doctor.

Jewel Anne and I got in the car and drove all the way to the station in silence. Not exactly what the books like to call "companionable silence" either. I walked her to her car waiting in the visitor's parking and held open her door for her. "Well," I said, as she slipped in behind the wheel.

"Well," she said, and started the engine.

"See you later," I said.

"No. Tonight's Friday. Don't forget you have plans with Glenda Sue."

"Oh, yeah. I almost did. Thanks." She smiled and drove off. It was a beginning.

ELEVEN

I WOULDA GOT STRAIGHT onto the Bell case when I got back, except something else came up. Something totally unexpected. It all came about because Bernie Hatcher's cousin (Bernie being the owner of the Chat and Chew), Myrtle Manchester, went to Greenesville, in Tejas County, to see her youngest daughter, Alice, who's been living over there with a guy her daddy doesn't like.

This was Myrtle's first time to visit because her husband, Ham, forbade her to go. But Myrtle was watching Oprah one day and got her feminist self-righteous anger up and decided she'd go visit her daughter if she damn well felt like it. No man was gonna tell her what she could or couldn't do. That "obey" stuff in the marriage ceremony only went so far, and anyway, most people were taking it out nowadays.

So, Myrtle went visiting in Greenesville and she and her daughter decided to go shopping at one of those ministorage places that had been turned into an arts-and-craft and antique mall. While there, they stopped by a place called Grandma's Cupboard, which was being run by what turned out to be a renegade offshoot of the fire department's Ladies' Auxiliary. According to Myrtle's story, everything in Grandma's Cupboard was made out of peaches. Peach pies, peach cobblers, peach preserves, peach compote, peach ice cream, spiced peaches, candied peaches, brandied peaches; you name it, if it coulda been made out of peaches, they had it. And Myrtle just happened to notice, through an open doorway to a back room of Grandma's Cupboard, case upon case of canned peaches.

Well, the Hatcher family is a close family, so immediately upon getting home from Greenesville, Myrtle calls up cousin Bernie and mentions Grandma's Cupboard. That had been the night before. On Friday morning, Bernie shows up ready to organize a posse to go to Tejas County, hang them renegade auxiliary women, and get back his stolen diet lunch special.

I came back from Dr. Marston's office and walked right, smack dab into the middle of it all. Dalton, bless his heart, was trying to handle Bernie as best he could. But, unfortunately, Dalton's best compares to other people's comatose periods.

After I got all the ugly details from Mr. Hatcher, I proposed that he go on back to the Chat and Chew and let me and Dalton handle it from there. He grumbled a bit but finally saw that I was right. Then I put in a call to Bill Williams in the Tejas County Sheriff's Department, and asked if he would kindly meet me over near Greenesville at Grandma's Cupboard.

Mrs. Norella Nash and her twin sister, Mrs. Corella Nash (they'd married the Nash brothers from Okila, Bertram and Ossie), both wearing lovely matching gingham dresses with lovely matching sun bonnets, were presiding over Grandma's Cupboard when Bill and I both drove up, almost at the same time. Him, me, and Dalton all walked into together. I brought Dalton along because this was, after all, his case.

Bill introduced himself to the two Mrs. Nashes and then introduced Dalton and myself, letting them know we were from Prophesy County. Norella, or it coulda been Corella, who the hell could tell, made a run for it, surprising the shit out of me and the other two alert peace officers. Who'd a' thought an eighty-year-old lady had it in her? Corella, on the other hand, or Norella, whichever, just stayed where she was and burst into tears. Bill and me looked at each other, trying to decide which one of us wanted to be seen chasing the other old lady. I finally decided to do it because I didn't have to live in this county.

So, anyway, I took off after the fleeing Mrs. Nash, who'd already made it to the end of the row of lease sheds and woulda made it to the street if her claw-footed cane hadn't got caught in some tall weeds. I just thanked God I didn't have to tackle her and end up breaking a hip—either hers or mine. She did manage to get the cane loose just as I got there and got it up almost high enough to hit me with before I wrestled it out of her surprisingly strong grip.

I escorted her back to Grandma's Cupboard while we locked the place up and then escorted the two ladies back to the Tejas County Sheriff's Department. I stayed with the ladies while Bill went out to round up the rest of the renegade Ladies' Auxiliary, all fourteen of 'em.

Dalton and I spent the rest of the day helping Bill take statements. And it all boiled down to this: the fire department got a new chief a couple of years ago, a young guy in his thirties. When he took over, his wife sorta took over the Ladies' Auxiliary, which is the God-given right of the wife of every fire chief of every volunteer fire department in the country. But in doing so, she managed to bring in a lot of younger women, and began sorta edging out the older ladies who'd comprised the Ladies' Auxiliary for the past thirty years. These ladies' husbands hadn't been volunteers for many years, but almost all of 'em had a son or grandson willing to risk his life over a barn fire.

One of the chief things the Ladies' Auxiliary did every year was have a big bake sale and jumble auction to raise money for the fire department. The renegade ladies decided the only way back into the inner circle was to make more money for the fire department than the auxiliary did. So they'd have their own damned bake sale, by God!

Mrs. Eugenia Blott's grandson owned the mini-storage place and gave them their space there. Now all they needed to do was come up with a product to sell. All of the sixteen ladies were on fixed incomes and couldn't afford to spend the money necessary to produce the large amount of baked goods required to beat the pants off the Ladies' Auxiliary. No one would admit, or could remember, whose idea it had been to start robbing grocery stores. They did remember, though, that someone thought it would be a good idea not to do it in their own backyard, so to speak, and that Prophesy County looked like pretty good pickin's.

The first place they hit they were just too scared to go much farther than the back door, and the closest thing worth stealing to that door was twelve cases of canned peaches. When they got back and started making their treats and selling them at the ministorage, the peach motif was such a hit that that became their speciality. The rest was purdee history.

When I got back to Prophesy County it was close to quitting time, but that doesn't seem to mean much in my line of work. Gladys met me at the door with an urgent message.

"That Bernblatt person's been trying to reach you all day."

"I'm all thrilled."

She shoved the messages in my hand. "You know," she said, "a body could get really tired of your brand of humor, Chief Deputy." She did a neat about-face and marched back to her part of the station. She was right, I knew she was right. But somehow, I just couldn't help myself.

There were five messages in all, all of them with the words "Urgent," "ASAP," "Immediately," etc., on them. So I decided, what the hey, and gave Bernblatt a call.

"Jesus Christ, it's about fucking time!" was his greeting.

"I been working."

"Yeah, I bet."

"What the hell's that supposed to mean?"

"Get your ass over to the Longbranch Inn quick!"

"Hey, I'm off duty. As of two minutes ago."

"I found the Colombian connection," he said, and hung up.

So, of course, I got in my '55 and headed for the Longbranch Inn. Worrying that maybe I'd been wrong all along and there was a Colombian connection and I'd missed it and I'd have Bernblatt to thank for solving the case. It wasn't a pleasant thought.

I parked in front of the inn and walked in the front doors. Bernblatt was pacing the foyer. "Jesus, I didn't think you'd ever get here. The guy could split on us any minute."

"Where?" I asked, my hand moving toward my gun and my palm beginning to sweat.

"In the kitchen."

"The kitchen?"

"Yeah, come on."

I followed him into the dining room, waving at my lady friend as I passed her filling up salt shakers at one of the tables, and moved with Bernblatt toward the door to the kitchen.

"You go in first," he whispered.

"Why?" I demanded.

"You've got the gun!"

"Oh."

I moved around him and edged the door open. There was a man with his back to me, bent over some dishes. "Hold it right there," I said. "Sheriff's department."

Jackie Hernandez spun around, almost dropping one of the Longbranch Inn special logo plates. The ones you get when you order one of their special sizzler T-bones.

I looked at Bernblatt. "This your Colombian?" I asked.

"Hey," Jackie said, "I ain't no Colombian! I'm an American! Jesus! I never been south a' Ardmore in my life!" His hands were still shaking from the scare of a gun pointed at him.

I holstered my gun and looked at Bernblatt. "Well," Bernblatt said, "he *looks* Colombian."

The scare had left him and Jackie was getting mad. "Hey, Milt, who is this sumbitch?"

"Sorry, Jackie," I said, taking Bernblatt by the shoulders and turning him around and shoving him out the door.

"How long have you known this guy?" Bernblatt demanded, not one to let go of an issue easily.

"I dated his mother," I said. "In high school."

"Oh" was as gracious as he was gonna get about it so I let it drop.

I got rid of Bernblatt and headed back to the dining room for Glenda Sue, ready as all get-out for our Friday night to begin. I knew my Saturday was gonna be spent working, what with picking up Mrs. Jacobsen from the Tulsa airport and dealing with all that. Dalton would be working, too, going by every single store that had been hit in the great peach rip-off and trying to talk them into not pressing charges. I figured it would be pretty bad to have every grandmother in Greenesville, Oklahoma, locked up.

Figuring I owed Glenda Sue, because of that screwed-up Wednesday night, not to mention almost shooting her restaurant's dishwasher, I headed straight to the VFW hall, no discussion required. The Friday night dance was in full swing when we got there. And I gotta say Glenda Sue was real good about it all. She never asked me to dance unless it was a slow tune. The lady has a lot of sensitivity.

But kissing my lady good-bye at the door of her trailer (it wasn't all that chaste, she was in her bathrobe, thank you very much!) wasn't to be the end of my exceedingly long day. Oh, no, not by a long shot. I got back to my house and had to park not behind just Bernblatt's rental, but that great big old shiny Cadillac as well. I sat in my car for a minute wondering if I really wanted to go inside my own house, or if it wouldn't just been more peaceful to lie down on the highway. The only thing that decided me on going in the house was that it began to rain. I figure God made the decision for me.

I went into the house and walked into the living room and almost burst out laughing. Bernblatt was sitting on one end of the couch, Harmon was sitting on the other, and Jewel Anne had taken my easy chair halfway across the room from 'em both. Good for you, girl, I thought. Show 'em who's boss.

Everybody stood up at my entrance. It was after one o'clock in the morning and I had to wonder how long they'd been sitting like that. I also had to wonder where Harmon's wife thought he might be at this hour. But, of course, that was none of my business.

"Evenin'," I called out.

"Evenin'," Harmon ventured.

"Hi," Bernblatt said.

"Milton." Jewel smiled sheepishly.

"Everybody enjoying their Friday night?" I asked, all innocent like.

Harmon looked down at his shoes, Bernblatt looked up at the ceiling fan, and Jewel just glared at me.

"Well, I'm off to bed," I said, and left them as they'd been.

By the time I got my drawers off, the storm was going full blast. Rain hitting the windows like an Uzi at a shopping mall. The wind whipped the trees, breaking off branches and scattering leaves I'd have to pick up. I'd just crawled under the covers when I heard a great crash, followed almost instantly by my sister yelling "Milton!"

I jumped out of the bed, pulled on my pants, grabbed my shoes, and headed down the stairs. Bernblatt was standing by the fireplace looking around with eyes bigger than the Longbranch Inn's Blue Plate Special. Harmon, though, a native Oklahoman, was staring out one of the windows at the storm.

"Somethin' over by the garage went down, Milt," he said, as I entered the room.

"Oh, my God!" Jewel said. "Leonard!"

"Hold on, little girl," I muttered, pulling on my shoes without socks, "don't go panicking till there's something to panic about." I went to the front door to open it just as Leonard came dashing in in his underwear.

"Jesus, Uncle Milt! Did you see that?" We both watched as a limb bigger than some trees scooted across in front of the door.

"How bad's your place?" I asked.

"Bad! A limb came in through the back window and crashed down on my CD player!"

And that's when I heard it. The rain slacked off, and behind it I could hear the great rumbling of a freight train headed our way. Only we didn't live anywhere near any tracks.

I looked at Harmon. "Get the kids! Upstairs!" He and Leonard ran up the stairs two at a time. I didn't have to speak to my sister. Her Oklahoma upbringing already had her in the kitchen, her tornado box in her hands. As she came lurching toward me with it, I called out to Bernblatt, "Get the damned box before she drops it!"

"What the hell's going on?" Bernblatt said, not having moved from the fireplace.

I grabbed the box, Bernblatt's arm, and headed for the back door, Jewel, Harmon, and the kids behind us. "A tornado, asshole," I told Bernblatt.

I opened the back door, fighting the wind for control. Bernblatt pulled away from me. "I'm not going out there!"

I could feel Jewel Anne push him from behind. "The storm cellar's out there, Marv! Move it!"

With me pulling and Jewel pushing we managed to get the dumb, Yankee asshole outside, and he even wised up enough finally to hold the box while I wrestled the storm cellar doors open. The night was black as pitch, but not so black I couldn't see my hundred-year-old oak tree bent almost to the ground by the wind. I stood back while Bernblatt went in first, helping Jewel and the kids down the stairs. A gust of wind caught the door as Harmon was going down, wrenching it from my hands and banging him on the head. He fell the ten steps down.

They were all safe inside, with me on the outside, holding on to the handle of the cellar door for dear life, wondering if it was all gonna end this way. Then I felt the door punching into my belly and finally realized they were trying to open it from down below.

I slid over to the side, releasing my grip on the door handle, exchanging it for a grip on the two-by-four frame of the doorway. I saw Bernblatt's face ease over the door frame and felt his arms tugging at me. Finally I let go of the two-by-four and slid headfirst down the stairs to the cellar, Bernblatt breaking my fall.

I sat up and looked around. For a little while anyway, sibling rivalry was over for my niece and nephews. Marlene and Carl huddled next to their big brother, who had protective arms around the two of them. Jewel was busy with a cold compress pressed to Harmon's head. I felt a shove from beneath me and heard Bernblatt say, with what little breath he had left, "Get the fuck off me." That's when I realized I was still sitting on him.

"Oh, sorry," I said, sliding off. "Everybody okay?"

"I think he'll be all right," Jewel said, meaning Harmon. We had to talk loud over the roar of the freight train bearing down on my house. My house. My beautiful crazy house. In my mind's eye I saw it exploding in a million pieces, whirling upward into the bowels of the twister and coming to rest in some crazy Oz. And then, for a minute, I felt just like Dorothy, because I remembered Evinrude. And realized he wasn't here with us. For a crazy second, I almost ran up the stairs and outside in search of my Toto. But being a grown man with a family and a responsible job, instead of a little girl with funny shoes, I stayed where I was, saying only "Goddamn it, we forgot the cat!" But even that bit of humanity ebbed away as a new thought hit me: I wondered if I'd made my last insurance payment.

It seemed like days that we sat there listening to the terror above us uprooting the world, the wind shrieking, the rain sounding more like a small boy outside the door, spraying us with automatic BB-gun fire. Inside the ancient shelter, which I'd never been in before, the wind from the outside was seeping in enough to cause little whirlwinds of dust and cobwebs to set us all to coughing.

This wasn't my first tornado, not by a long shot. But you never get used to it. Never get used to the ravages of nature, the pure terror of something so completely out of control. I remembered my daddy, when I was a kid, standing on the front porch watching a twister coming toward the house.

"Your mama and the baby in the cellar?" he'd asked.

"Yes, sir." He'd nodded and stood there for a minute, smoking a cigarette. I was fourteen, nearly a man, but standing there with him, watching that tornado twist its way toward us, was the most terrifying thing I'd ever done in my life. Worse even than asking for my first date. But I knew I couldn't move. I couldn't run for the safety of the cellar. Watusi warriors have their rituals of manhood, Jewish boys get bar mitzvahed, us Oklahoma boys knew we were truly men only when we could stand with our daddies and watch a twister heading to kill us.

Finally, with the wind whipping the branches of trees, tearing the blooms of Mama's newly blossomed flowers, Daddy smashed his cigarette out with the heel of his boot and said, oh, so calmly, "Well, guess we'd best head for the cellar." It took every ounce of courage I could muster to walk, not run.

Although it seemed like hours, it wasn't all that long before it moved on. We stayed in the cellar, though, until it was calm, until we could hear the rain making little rat-a-tat-tat sounds on the cellar door.

I opened the door and peeked out first, as was my right and duty as homeowner. It didn't look too bad. The house was still standing. I could see my windowed room on the second floor, all windows intact. I looked to the left at the garage, or where the garage was supposed to be. It was gone. Along with Leonard's room above. We all climbed out and, in the light rain, began to inspect the damage. The garage, as I said, was but a distant memory, as were the stable and corral. The screened-in front porch was also a thing of the past. But the house itself was intact. Not even a window broken.

Bernblatt's rental car was turned over in the driveway, and Harmon's Cadillac had a nice-size tree limb as a hood ornament. Jewel's car, which had been in the garage, could be dimly seen down in the valley behind the house. My '55 was the only thing intact. I knew then that the song I sang as a child had been correct: Jesus loved me.

We got everybody back in the house while I stood where my porch once was and surveyed the damage. After looking long and hard at where the stable and corral used to be, I went back into the house.

Everybody was standing there looking at me. "Kids," I said, "now that we have nowhere to put horses, how'd you like a swimming pool instead?"

"Awright!"

"Milton, that's a great idea! We'll go halvsies!"

"Mom, can I get a bikini?"

We got Carl and Marlene back in bed and found Evinrude asleep on my bed, totally oblivious to his near death. I went to the phone and found it dead and headed out to the '55 and my radio. I got the station and told them what had happened.

"I'm heading on down to Falls End now to see if Haywood's okay. Just to be safe, why don't you get an ambulance to meet me that end?"

Wearing a too-big pair of my jeans, Leonard joined Harmon, Bernblatt, and myself as we got in my car and headed down Mountain Falls Road to survey the damage. I headed first to Fall's End, because Haywood Hunter was the only human besides my family still living full time on the mountain. Halfway there, we had to stop for a tree blocking the road. I turned around and went the other way, planning on going back down the mountain on the other side to the highway, and up the highway to the second entrance to Fall's End. Unfortunately, there was a house blocking the road. The whole thing. Picked up and set down slanchwise across Mountain Falls Road. I recognized it as the former home of the artist who'd moved out two years before.

I backed the '55 up as far as Billy Moulini's driveway and turned it around, heading back to where the tree had stopped us. From there, we all got out and walked. It was a big tree and we had to walk several feet off the road, slipping and sliding in the ditch to get around it. Once around, it was still half a mile to Fall's End.

Using my heavy-duty policeman's flashlight, I led the way down the road, half afraid of what I'd find.

TWELVE

THE NIGHT WASN'T AS BLACK as it had first seemed. As our eyes adjusted we barely needed the flashlight; the clouds in the sky reflected their own light. I mainly used the flashlight on the road, as a way of preparing ourselves for broken limbs, downed trees, or maybe even a flying house or two. At this point, anything was a possibility.

The half-mile to Haywood's place was covered in good time, since it was all downhill. But once we turned into his road, without the aid of the flashlight, we could see the damage. Fall's End was underwater. The small dam that had kept the water in the pool at the end of the falls had obviously been destroyed, flooding the whole area. Half of the log-cabin store was demolished. The other half, which interested me, was still standing, although water had risen to above the windows. That half interested me because that was the half behind which Haywood's sleeping quarters were.

I went the rest of the way down the incline and into the water.

"Snakes, Uncle Milt!" Leonard yelled behind me.

"No snakes this time a year," I answered, rushing headlong into the water, trying not to think that I'd also remarked that we didn't get tornados this time of year. I just prayed God I'd be half right.

I heard the others splashing in behind me. Turning, I handed the flashlight to Leonard. "You stay on high ground and shine the light in front of us so we'll know where we're going, okay?"

"Yeah, Uncle Milt."

Then I yelled, "Haywood! You in there? Haywood!"

After walking in about ten feet into what used to be the parking area of Fall's End, I found myself on tiptoe in order to keep my nose outa the water. I felt an arm come under mine and lift me slightly. "Hold on to me. I think I can walk it," Bernblatt said. Harmon, who was barely an inch taller than me, hooked on to Bernblatt's other arm and we dog-paddled our way to the front steps of the store. There was a slight dip right before the entrance and all three of us went down, coming up to shrieks of "Uncle Milt! Uncle Milt!"

I found a foothold on the porch step and pulled myself and the others up, calling "It's okay, boy. We're all okay."

I leaned against the porch railing for a minute and looked at Harmon, who'd been working his tail off for somebody else's family. "None of my business,

Harmon, but ain't you worried none about your wife and kids?"

He looked at me for a half a second and then looked out over the flood water. "They're in Oklahoma City with my in-laws. Left two days ago."

All I said was "Oh," then turned back to the business at hand.

"Haywood!" I yelled. "You there, old man?"

"In here!" I heard distantly. "And don't call me old man!"

The door to the store was jammed shut. We pushed and pulled and tried lifting it up and pushing it down but it wouldn't budge. Bernblatt tried ramming a shoulder into it but I coulda told him that wouldn't work. Only works on TV. The best way to open a locked door is by kicking it with the heel of your shoe right at the locking apparatus. But as the water was over chest deep, all kicking would be done in slow motion and wasn't worth the effort.

I felt around the front of the store until I found one of the windows. As a good-size two-by-four floated by, I grabbed it and used it to break through the window, clearing the shards of glass away.

"Haywood, we're coming!" I yelled.

"Won't do you no good to come that way, Milt! The door 'tween the office and the house's done blocked off or I'd already be out."

"How you doing?" I called.

"How'd you be doing if you were seventy years old and been treading water near on an hour, boy?"

"That deep in there?"

"No, I just like treading water! Don't be a jack-ass!"

I turned to the others. "Might not be all that deep. Haywood's a couple inches shorter than me."

"I'm the tallest," Bernblatt said. "Let me." He went underwater and through the window and disappeared. Finally we saw his head bob up. "The goddamn floor's gone! No wonder he's treading water! It's a good foot over my head in here!"

I turned and hollered back up to Leonard, up at the top of the incline. "Boy, get to the highway and down to the first entrance. Be just our luck the ambulance will go in that way and get stuck. Direct them in the back entrance and get 'em here fast. Okay?"

"Yeah, Uncle Milt!"

"And, Leonard, be careful!"

I don't know if he heard me, because he was already gone.

"Now what?" Bernblatt asked, having gotten himself through the window and back on the porch.

"Well, we could try going around to the back. Maybe there's a way in there."

"It's going to be over our heads," Bernblatt said. "And for some reason, there's an undertow, even inside the store."

"We'll just find us some handholds on the log walls and hand-walk our way around."

They both nodded their heads and we started, me in the lead. Ain't that always the way? Have a simple little job in law enforcement and everybody thinks you got to be the authority in times of trouble. That gets on my nerves.

It wasn't so much an undertow as it was the strength of white water rapids as we hand-walked our way toward the back. We kept close together, grabbing each other as a hand would slip. Luckily, no six hands slipped at the same time. Halfway to the back, something hit my left leg hard, shoving me into Harmon who was right behind me. The pain in my leg was unbelievable, but once Bernblatt got us both upright again, we kept going. What else was there to do?

With my right leg, I began tapping the walls, listening for the sound of glass as opposed to log. Almost to the back, I heard the sound I was listening for.

"There's a window here," I said. "Haywood!" I shouted. "Can you hear me?"

There was a muffled, very tired-sounding "Yeah" from the other side of the logs.

"Shit," I said, "that old man can't hold on much longer."

"Where's that two-by-four?" Harmon asked.

"I didn't bring it with me."

"Why the hell not?" Bernblatt demanded.

"Because I needed two goddamn hands to get back here!"

"Come on, you two," Harmon said. "We gotta work together." Bernblatt and I did work together, at least in glaring daggers at Harmon. Nobody likes the voice of reason at a time like this.

"Well, kick the damn window in," Bernblatt said.

"You kick it in! I only got one leg working right now and I'd like to keep it!"

"Jesus, the brave deputy!"

I took a swing at Bernblatt around Harmon's back, only managing to lose my grip and go under the black water. Harmon picked me up by the scruff of the neck. I managed to get my hands back in the grooves of the logs and balanced myself with one foot on either side of the window. My left leg didn't feel up to supporting me while I kicked with my right, and I figured the left leg was ruined anyway, why not use it? So, bracing myself, I called out to Haywood, "Get away from the window! I'm gonna kick it in!"

Distantly I heard, "Yeah, okay!"

I tried not to think about the thick socks I wasn't wearing as I smashed my foot through the glass just as Bernblatt handed me a tree branch passing by in the water. "Here, use this," he said. I didn't use it to bash his head in, which just goes to show what an incredibly righteous person I really am.

Using the limb, I cleared the shards of glass out of the window. "Haywood, you hear me?"

"Clear as a bell!"

"Can you swim over toward me?"

"Milt, I surely wish I could. But I don't believe I have it in me."

I turned to the others. "Take off your belts and string 'em together. If I go in there after him, I wanna know we're both coming back out!"

With both Harmon and Bernblatt hanging on, I strapped the three belts into one of my belt loops and went down and through the window, coming up in complete darkness and hitting my head on what I finally identified as a light fixture. Haywood had been treading water for over an hour in a space about two feet from the ceiling. I figured Jesus must love that old reprobate, too.

"Haywood, talk to me so I can find you."

"Over here, Milt. This way. You coming?"

I pulled on my belt leash and dog-paddled toward the sound of his voice. "Stretch your hand out, Haywood, toward my voice."

"I am, you idiot!"

"Keep talking!"

"So, whatja think of this weather?"

"Very funny!" Our hands slapped as we both waved toward each other, then came to rest in the other's grasp. I pulled Haywood to me.

"I got him!" I called toward the window, and felt an immediate tug on the belt. "Not so goddamn fast! Keep it tight! I'll come to you!"

Hand over hand I pulled us toward the window, Haywood with his arms around my neck, resting his legs for the first time in an hour. But getting the old man to go under the water and through the window was another chore. We argued for about a minute, then I pushed his head down until I felt one of the others grabbing him. He came up sputtering and cursing.

"I'll get you for this, Kovak! You tried to kill me!"

"I just saved your goddamned life, you old bastard!"

Harmon and Bernblatt kept him between them as they hand-walked back to the porch, not so much for his protection, I think, as mine. The old man was surely pissed about the dip.

Once on the porch I asked Haywood if he was okay. "Okay? Okay! Almost drowned to death and you ask me if I'm okay! You got your nerve, boy, you surely do!"

"Haywood, that was the only way outta there!"

He didn't answer. Bernblatt coaxed the old man onto his back and walked him up to higher ground.

Harmon and I swam in their wake until we could touch.

We all collapsed on the soggy but above-water ground, and then heard the sounds of the sirens wailing toward us. "About fuckin' time," Bernblatt managed to say before he fell back, exhausted.

Paramedics checked everybody out, with Leonard hanging over their shoulders watching their every move, and felt Haywood was the only one needing to go to the hospital. His one-hour stint of treading water had all but totally exhausted the old man. We watched the ambulance's departure, weaving its way around fallen limbs on its way to the highway. Then we hitched our own ride with A.B., the night deputy who'd taken the call. We drove out to the highway, then north to the first entrance to Mountain Falls Road and got as far as the artist's residence, which was still sitting in the middle of the road.

"Well, don't that beat all?" A.B. said. The rest of us merely nodded.

According to A.B., Mountain Falls Road had been the only area in the county hit. We thanked him for the ride and wearily walked the rest of the way to the house. An anxious Jewel Anne greeted us. Glancing at the clock, I grimaced at the time. Four-thirty A.M. In less than six hours I needed to be on the highway to Tulsa, on my way to the airport and Mrs. Jacobsen.

I went upstairs with Leonard, who'd be sharing space with his brother for awhile, and we both stripped off our drenched clothes, pulled on clean and crawled into bed, not wondering once what Jewel was gonna do with her two dates.

THIRTEEN

"I WISH YOU'D KNOWN my daughter," Mrs. Jacobsen said. "The woman you knew—she wasn't Annette. She was just some woman living in other people's houses...living other people's lives. My Annette—she was—"

I took one hand off the steering wheel and squeezed Mrs. Jacobsen's hand. "Yes, ma'am," I said. We sat in silence for a while, with me thinking about what she'd said and feeling it hitting home. Other people's houses. Yeah, I knew about that. That was my job. Going in other people's houses, looking at the places where items stolen had stood, looking at places where bloody bodies had lain. I knew all about other people's houses. I'd even lived in a few. My parents' house, my wife's house, and now, though at first it had been mine, my sister's house. And something made me wanna burst into tears. Because there was no way I, or anyone, could understand what Lois had been going through. I felt the tears in the back of my throat, the burning, and the knot in my scrotum the size of a softball. Course, I hadn't slept much and I'd just finished one two-hour drive and was on my way to making my second. I was just tired. That's all.

After a while she started talking. "I was lucky. I had great kids. My husband walked out on us when Annette was three years old. And never paid a bit of child support or anything. So I had to go to work. Larry, that's my son, was two years older than Annette. They stayed with a neighbor down the street while I went to work. I was a waitress at Howard Johnson's for thirty-two years. Thirty-two years of standing on my feet all day long and taking crap off strangers. But after the kids got older, when I'd get home supper would be on the table, a pot of coffee on the stove, and all I'd have to do would be lie down on the couch and put my feet up. Sometimes Annette would even rub my feet for me, when she could see it'd been a real bad day. And they'd both sit with me and tell me about what had happened at school, and who said what about who, and all that. Yeah, I was lucky. I liked my kids. Not everybody can say that, especially when their kids are teenagers. But mine, both of them, never gave me any trouble. They made good grades, and Larry even got a scholarship to a junior college. Even though he only went one year. At least he made it to college. First one in the family to make it to college. After Annette graduated, I got her a job at the Howard Johnson's while

she went to school nights to learn bookkeeping.
That's where she met David.''

She turned to me and smiled and I smiled back.
She was happy remembering and I didn't want to
have her stop. We had a whole two hours for her to
remember, before reality reared its ugly head.

"He was teaching drafting at the same night
school. He'd already gotten out of college with his
engineering degree, and he was just waiting for his
commission to come in from the marines, so he was
teaching nights. They met in the coffee shop next to
the school. After class. And then they started meeting there every night Annette had a class until he finally asked her out. Seemed then like it took forever.
We'd talk about it. She was nineteen and so ready for
her life to start! So eager! Finally he did. Ask her
out, I mean. They went to the movies. They went to
see *Rocky*. The first one, remember?''

"Yes, ma'am, I sure do.''

"My son Larry took me to see it after Annette kept
raving about it. I thought it was a little farfetched
myself. Anyway, that was the first night I met David. Very impressive young man. A lot of ambition.
His father had worked night shift at a factory, but he
was older when they had David and was already re-
tired by the time David got to college. So David had
to pay his own way through. Working two or three

jobs sometimes. And after they started dating steady, poor Annette kept asking *me* why he never proposed! I figured he was waiting for his commission to come through, or to get a good job. Any boy with as much ambition as David wasn't going to saddle himself with a wife until he was financially ready. Any fool could see he was madly in love with Annette. But I guess a girl in love is as big a fool as they come. Annette never believed me when I'd tell her. The only person she'd believe was David. They went together for three months, then Annette broke up with him!''

She paused, and looked at me as if for comment. Always obliging, I said, ''No kidding?''

''Yes! I always thought it was to make him jealous. I still do. She started dating this other boy—God, I don't even remember his name!—but she was never serious about him. The marines finally contacted David, then he comes marching over to the house. The other boy was in the living room with Annette and I was in the kitchen—I'm shameless, Deputy, I listened to the whole thing!''

I smiled in encouragement.

''Anyway, he knocks on the front door and when Annette opens it, he sees this other boy sitting on the couch. He says, 'Annette, I need to talk with you.' She says, 'I have company right now.' He says, 'I

don't give a damn! I want to talk with you now!'
Well, Annette gets huffy and starts to slam the door
in his face, and he just pushes his way right in. And
this other boy jumps up from the couch and I'm
thinking, Oh, my God, they're going to wreck my
living room!''

We both laugh.

"And this other boy says something like 'What the
hell do you think you're doing?' and David says,
'You stay out of this, asshole!'" Turning to me, she
said, "Excuse my language."

"No problem."

"Anyway, Annette jumps in, saying 'David, you
have no right!' And he grabs both her arms and
looking her right in the face, he says, 'I have every
right! I love you! I want to marry you!'"

Mrs. Jacobsen stopped her story and looked at
me. "Isn't that the most romantic thing you've ever
heard?"

I nodded my head. "Yes, ma'am, it surely is."

She leaned her head back against the headrest.
"Just like a romance novel."

She was silent for a minute and, worried that she
might think I wasn't interested, I said, "So what'd
that other boy do?"

She started, then laughed. "Oh, he was ready to
punch David out except before he could, Annette

threw her arms around David and yells 'Yes!' at the top of her lungs. The next day somebody emptied a garbage can on our front porch and I always figured it was that other boy, but we could never prove it.''

We sat in silence for a while, then she said, "It was a beautiful wedding. Larry gave Annette away. She didn't even try to find her father, which I was grateful for, though, of course, I never said anything. I figured it was up to her. They got married right after David was through with OTS. He was in his dress blues and they had an honor guard and everything. It was lovely. They were a beautiful couple, Deputy. And very happy. Annette was twenty when they married. It seemed like it took forever, but David didn't want to start a family until he was established. So when he was promoted to captain, that's when Annette got pregnant. She was twenty-seven when Alan was born."

"Alan?"

She looked at me. "My oldest grandson."

"Oh." I looked away when I said, "I know him as Bill, Jr."

She didn't say anything, just looked away. Reality's ugly head had risen. We rode in silence for a way.

Finally I asked, "What about Mr. and Mrs. Tapp? I mean, I called them the same night I called you, but they didn't seem interested...."

She shook her head. "They're both drinkers, you know."

I clucked my tongue. "No, ma'am, I didn't know that."

"Of their four children, David was the only one who'd amounted to anything. The two girls married, one to a bum, the other to a revivalist preacher who truly believes poverty is a virtue! And the other son, Conrad, Lord! He's been in more trouble than you can imagine! Drugs, gambling, women..."

"That can be hard on a family," I ventured.

"You'd think they'd appreciate David! But no! They did not! Just expected him to take care of everybody! Half the time David was bailing Conrad out of jail, or buying groceries for Lani, the sister married to the bum, or sending checks to Angie, the other sister, so she could buy clothes for her kids! And always, like clockwork, giving checks to his folks! Sometimes I'd get so mad! And then I'd say something to Annette about it and feel just awful about it afterward."

She sat quietly thinking and, in a moment, spoke again. "Annette called me on a Tuesday. The day after she testified at the trial. They'd kept the whole family in a hotel during the trial. She called me and asked me to meet her that night at her home. That's when I found out they'd have to go away. I thought my heart would break. I think maybe it did actually.'' She heaved a great sigh. ''The people were there from the U.S. Marshal's office, helping them pack up the few things they could take with them. David had called his folks, too, and they got there a little after me. God, Deputy, they threw a fit! You wouldn't believe it! Both of them drunk as skunks, anyway. Accusing David of running out on his responsibilities! As far as I could see, his only real responsibilities were to Annette and the children! But not to hear them tell it! Then they started in on Annette! Saying she'd done all this just to take David away from his family! Can you believe it? And then they started telling David how he shouldn't be married to a woman who'd get into this kind of trouble! Calling my daughter all sorts of nasty names! I just went crazy and hit Mr. Tapp full in the face with my purse!''

I laughed. ''Good for you,'' I said.

She smiled. ''Well, it was terrible, really. I should never have done that, but, God, the things that man was saying about my child! Anyway, they both said point blank that if David left, he would be out of their lives forever and they'd never do another thing for him. As if they ever did! And then they took them. The Marshal. They took Annette and David and the children in this station wagon, and that's the last I ever saw of them.''

She grew quiet then, and we drove in silence the rest of the way. I knew I should probably keep her talking, but I was too tired to think of anything to say. My experience of the night before was wearing on me. My left leg was black and blue from my knee to my ankle from whatever it was that had hit me in the water. My shoulders ached from the long hand-over-hand walk along the log-cabin wall, and I had other aches and pains that didn't seem logical but hurt all the same.

I'd called the hospital before I'd left the house that morning to check on Haywood. According to the nurse who answered, who'd been a classmate of Jewel's and was more than willing to spill her guts to me, not only a sheriff's deputy but the brother of a friend as well, Haywood was giving them more trouble than three ordinary patients. He complained about the food, the medicine, and the nurses, and refused to use a bedpan, threatening one nurse he'd aim at her eyeballs if she didn't let him up to use the facilities. I figured he was doing okay.

We got into Longbranch at a little after three-thirty. I took her straight to the Longbranch Inn where I checked her in, waiting downstairs in the café, talking to my lady love, while she readied herself to go to the hospital and identify the bodies.

Dr. Jim had been real good about hiding the bodies. In my last conversation with him, I'd found out Jackson Taylor had been hanging around almost steady, trying to get to the bodies before Mrs. Jacobsen could get there and identify them. And I, probably just to be ornery to both Taylor and Bernblatt, had called every news service I could think of to let them know they might want to be at the hospital around four o'clock. I didn't want Taylor thinking he could bamboozle Mrs. Jacobsen. I didn't want him thinking he could get away with one damn thing. And I also figured Bernblatt could use a little competition. I mean, that's the American way, isn't it?

I was half afraid that the news services wouldn't pay any heed to a small-town deputy sheriff like myself, but at four o'clock, when Mrs. Jacobsen and I strolled down the corridor toward Dr. Jim's office, I was gratified and a little overwhelmed to see my fears had been for naught. There were about a dozen people standing outside the doors, only two of 'em being Jackson Taylor and my friend Bernblatt, both of 'em giving me looks that could've injured my soul, if I hadn't been an upstanding, card-carrying member of the Longbranch First Baptist Church and shielded by righteousness. Dalton was standing guard at the door, his bulk, if not his authority, keeping the crowd out.

All the news service people looked a little mystified and a little bored, until one of 'em recognized Mrs. Jacobsen from all the pictures they'd taken of the family at the trial of Eddie Cowan, and the word spread fast. Questions were flying fast and furious as we pushed through to the doors.

"Mrs. Jacobsen will make a statement in a minute," I told the crowd. "No questions until she's done what she's come for." We pushed through the doors, leaving the crowd on the other side.

Dr. Jim. had done his best making the bodies presentable. They were all laid out in a row, hospital-green sheets covering them. Seeing those five bodies, all in a row like that, starting from big with David/Bill and ending with little at the baby, Mrs. Jacobsen almost lost her footing, grabbing my arm to keep from keeling over.

"I'm sorry, ma'am," I said low, "so sorry."

She held tight to my arm and I walked her over to the second body, the body of her daughter. Dr. Jim removed the sheet and I put my arm around Mrs. Jacobsen's waist to hold her steady. She looked for a long time, then quietly reached out a hand and smoothed the hair off her child's forehead.

"Yes, Deputy. I identify this as the body of my daughter, Annette Jacobsen Tapp."

Dr. Jim covered Lois and went to her husband's body, uncovering the face. Mrs. Jacobsen looked at him, then looked quizzically at me. "This is David?"

"Isn't it?" I asked, my belly feeling like it just got punched.

"Well . . . yes . . . but . . . he looks awful!"

I restrained myself from commenting that he'd been dead for two weeks and none of us would look too good under those circumstances.

"He looks so heavy! He must have gained weight. And he looks ten years older than the last time I saw him! How could that be?"

She looked at her son-in-law, the man she knew as impressively ambitious, a family man on the go, the man I knew as an out-of-work mechanic and heavy boozer. And I had to agree: How could that be?

Even though I told her it wasn't necessary, she insisted on looking at each of the grandchildren. Her tears were flowing freely by this point, and when she got to the baby, the baby she'd never known, she picked the little girl up in her arms and held her against her breast, nuzzling her lifeless hair with her cheek and cooing to her. Dr. Jim and I stood by, and even that old coot had a tear in his eye. My first indication that he was, after all, human.

When she was ready, after she'd dried her eyes and squared her shoulders, we went through the doors to the corridor outside. Jackson Taylor eased up on her and began to whisper in her ear. To my delight, she pushed him away, saying "I'll say anything I damned well please to the press. You can't shut me up and don't you even try, young man!" I nodded to Dalton, who took Taylor by the arm and escorted him to the edge of the crowd, holding on to him so he wouldn't try to bolt and run. You never can tell what a fed's gonna do.

I spoke first. "This is Mrs. Barbara Jacobsen, for those of you who don't know. She came here today at my request to identify the bodies of her daughter and her daughter's family. Mrs. Jacobsen?"

She cleared her throat then spoke. "I have identified the bodies of my daughter and her husband, Annette and David Tapp, and of their three children. I've held my peace for three years now, but now I'm talking. Three years ago my daughter called me from Shreveport, Louisiana, where the Witness Protection Program had placed them, telling me that because of the death of Eddie Cowan, the WPP had decided they no longer needed to be in the program. But because of the nature of Mr. Cowan's death, and the threat it caused her family, my daughter and her husband felt they were still in danger from the Colombian drug smugglers. They pleaded with the WPP to reinstate them, but they were told that rules were rules, et cetera. At that time, I sent them what money I could. For three years now, they've been on their own, running from the butchers the WPP wouldn't protect them from. I'm not sure at this point what killed my family, but I hold the WPP entirely responsible." She pointed dramatically at Jackson Taylor, who looked small next to Dalton, in more ways than one.

Then the questions started, all at once and at the top of lungs. "One at a time!" I yelled. "Hold up your hand and you'll be recognized!" I figured if the President could do it that way, so could Milton Kovak.

Every hand in the place shot up, including Bernblatt's. Figuring I owed him one, I called on him first. "Deputy," he said, "could you please tell the press corps how you stumbled on the fact that this dead family you had could be the Tapp family from North Carolina?"

I smiled sweetly and said, "Good police work."

FOURTEEN

I INVITED MRS. JACOBSEN over for dinner that night and with her insistence on helping in the kitchen, dinner was almost edible. Bernblatt had finagled his way to a dinner invite through my sister, and thus managed an exclusive interview. Of course, he wasn't speaking to me, which I found just jim-dandy. After Mrs. Jacobsen's interview, the only person speaking to me had been Jackson Taylor. And what he had to say was meant not to be pleasant.

"Deputy," he'd said, his shit-eating grin a distant memory, "I hope to hell you got no aspirations for higher office. Because you just shot your wad. You're gonna be a no-account, small-time county deputy for the rest of your fucking life!"

Me being me and all, I'd just smiled sweetly and said, "Thank you very much."

After dinner, Mrs. Jacobsen got out a family album she'd brought with her. We all sat down on the couch to look at pictures of her dead family. There were pictures of the two older kids as babies, with a happy mom and dad looking down. Lois was easily recognizable, but I finally understood Mrs. Jacobsen's initial reluctance on identifying Bill. David Tapp and Bill Bell looked enough alike to have been distant cousins. David, lean, clear-eyed, his hair neatly trimmed, his casual clothes expensive and well maintained, looked little like Bill, who was overweight, bleary-eyed, with a constant three-day growth of beard, his clothing sloppy with indifference. I couldn't help but wonder what giving up his ordered life had cost him.

Toward the end of the album, I found out. I found out just what it had cost him. It was Christmas in the photos and the whole family was there. Mrs. Jacobsen, her son Larry and his wife and child, and Lois and her family. The photos showed the kids opening gifts, the little girl with a big doll, the boy with a baseball bat, and also photos of the others with their presents. Lois opening a big box. And Bill holding up a bathrobe. A red flannel bathrobe.

"What's this?" I asked.

Mrs. Jacobsen turned to me. "Oh, that was my gift to David that year. You'd be surprised how cold it can get in Raleigh in the winter. He really loved that bathrobe."

I took a deep breath. "Mrs. Jacobsen, would you recognize that robe if you saw it again?"

She thought for a moment. "Well, I suppose I would. Why?"

I didn't answer directly, because all of a sudden I remembered that magazine I'd found on one of my first searches of the Bell house. I excused myself to Mrs. Jacobsen and hightailed it out to my car, finding the magazine in the trunk where I'd thrown it the day I'd found it. I brought it back into the house.

Opening the magazine to the page that had been marked, I showed the picture of Grady Grimes to Mrs. Jacobsen and asked if she knew who it was.

Mrs. Jacobsen looked for just a minute and then laughed. "I sure do know who this is! Little Grady! Well, he certainly has done well for himself in four years. David hired him straight out of school about three years before they had to leave. He was one of these super-smart kids with no common sense. David used to call him that"—she pointed at the red-inked words "Fuck up!!!" written on the page—"all the time. When David said it it was almost like an endearment. But I'm glad to see they finally finished the project."

"What project's that?" I asked.

She pointed at the caption. "That coolant system. David worked on that for five years. It was his baby."

"And this fuck-up, excuse me, Grady Grimes, gets the patent on it and a vice presidency to boot?"

Mrs. Jacobsen looked up from the magazine, tears in her eyes. "That probably didn't sit real well with David."

"Probably not, Mrs. Jacobsen. Would you mind coming with me for a minute? Marv, you, too."

Marv nodded and helped Mrs. Jacobsen up. We put on our jackets for the cool evening and headed for my '55. I had wanted to avoid taking her to Lois's home. Had seen no reason to expose the mother to the horrors of her daughter's life. But now there was no getting out of it.

I tried warning her before we got there of what she would see. But there's no way to warn of that. The living room itself was like a physical blow to her. The smells had died down, but they were still there. The only light in the room was the overhead, which glared brightly on the living room, exposing the filth to the mother's eye. She reached for my arm for support and stared around her at her daughter's home.

"This isn't Annette's house," she said. It was a statement of fact. Of knowledge. This couldn't possibly be her daughter's home. Therefore, it was not.

"I'm sorry, Mrs. Jacobsen," I said. "I didn't want you to have to see this, but..."

She shook her head and a sob broke through her lips. "This isn't my daughter's house," she said in a harsh whisper.

I walked her briskly into the master bedroom, having Bernblatt go before us and shut the other doors so she couldn't see any more than she had to. Once in the master bedroom, I went directly to the dirty pile of clothes, where the red flannel bathrobe still sat on top. I held it up to her. I suppose it had little resemblance to the once-immaculate robe, now stained and tattered, but Mrs. Jacobsen looked at the label and said, "Yes, this is it."

I sat down heavily on the bed, wondering at my own stupidity. I'd *assumed* the robe had been Lois's. My wife had a blue robe just like it. But it hadn't been. It had been Bill's.

I cleared my throat and looked up at Mrs. Jacobsen. "Your daughter didn't kill herself," I said.

Mrs. Jacobsen sat down beside me. "I already knew that, Deputy."

I looked at Bernblatt. "And it wasn't any damned Colombians either."

"Okay," he said, staring at me like I'd lost my mind.

I took both of Mrs. Jacobsen's hands in mine. "You can see how bad things had gotten for Lo—Annette." She nodded her head. "She met a young

man who worked at the bank where she did. They fell
in love. They kept a little place over by a lake near
here. The place was immaculate. Beautiful. Not like
this at all. The reason I found out about that
place''—and here I looked at the floor because I felt
a fool and unable to face either of them—''was because I found receipts for the rental of it in that red
bathrobe. I thought the robe was Annette's. But it
was David's. I figure now he musta found those receipts and confronted her with 'em. Maybe she con-
fessed. I dunno. The boy told me he and Annette
planned on taking the kids and running off to
Houston together in January. Maybe she told Bill—
David—that. I dunno. Or maybe he just figured it all
out. Whatever the reason, I can understand how he
musta felt.'' I looked up at Mrs. Jacobsen. ''When
you saw him, you said how different he seemed.
Well, ma'am, he was different. He'd given up everything for Annette. The only jobs he'd been holding
lately were mechanic jobs and them not for long. As
I understand it, he drank so much he passed out almost every night. I can see him thinking he'd done all
this for Annette, and here she was getting ready to
run out on him. Add to that what we saw in that
magazine—his project . . . his patent—being taken
over by somebody he considered a fuck-up, the vice
presidency going to somebody else when it could

have been his. Now he finds out not only has he lost the vice presidency, but he's getting ready to lose Annette and the kids, too."

I got up and walked into the living room, the others following. "Dr. Jim said there was a crack on her head when he did the autopsy. He couldn't tell, though, how old it was. Could have been up to twenty-four hours before her death. I don't think so. I think David hit her that night. Knocked her unconscious, then he carried her out here." I walked to the door to the garage and opened it, turning on the light for all to see the car still sitting there. "And puts her in the car and starts the engine." I pulled the door to and walked to Bill's easy chair. "Then he closes the door and comes here and sits down with his beer and watches TV. By then he's probably too drunk to notice"—I walked back to the door and pushed it with a finger, seeing it open wide—"that the door wasn't latched properly. He probably planned on finding her body in the morning and being the grieving widower, but instead that door killed him and it killed the kids."

Mrs. Jacobsen's knees got wobbly and Bernblatt put his arms around her to support her. "Can you prove any of this?" he asked.

I shook my head. "Probably not. But I sure as hell am gonna fight it going down as a suicide. Annette didn't deserve for that to be her epitaph."

Mrs. Jacobsen said, "Poor David," and burst into tears.

That Monday the bodies were released to Mrs. Jacobsen and taken by hired ambulance to the Tulsa airport for their last flight home. Mrs. Jacobsen hugged me and kissed my cheek, thanking me and telling me she'd appreciate what I could do about getting the verdict as anything but suicide, but she'd understand if it ended up going down that way. There was a small life insurance policy through the bank that wouldn't pay off on suicide, but I don't think that was as much her concern as her daughter's honor. I promised to do what I could, not really knowing how it would end up.

Monday afternoon, at the station, I got a call from Billy Moulini. "You ain't gonna believe this," he said.

"What's that, Billy?"

"The Metropolis Developing Corporation out of Houston, Texas, has decided the Mountain Falls area ain't as choice as it once was. They had a little option in their contract and have voided their deals with Haywood and that artist fella."

"Why?"

"Why? 'Cause God in his wisdom decided to re-arrange the landscape. It would be, and I'm quoting the damned lawyers now, 'cost prohibitive' to get the pool back to its original shape."

"Well, that's fine and dandy for you and me, Billy, but what about poor Haywood? He was planning on retiring on that money."

"Ah, hell, I already made him an offer. Not as big as them condo people was gonna give him, but enough to last out his days in a little style. And I also made an offer on that artist fella's place. Less the cost of hauling off the house, which the county just shoved off to the side of the road! Anyway, all's well that ends well."

I smiled and thanked him and hung up, and be-gan to wonder how long it would be before Billy Moulini decided he wanted all of the mountain, not just four-fifths.

When I got home that evening, Bernblatt was in the living room arguing with my sister. "You don't belong in a place like this!"

"It's where I was born, Marv."

They both turned toward me when they heard my entrance.

"Hi, there," I said, all grins.

"Hi, yourself." Jewel grinned back at me. Bern-blatt just glared. He walked past me to the front door. Turning to Jewel, he said, "I'll be at the Longbranch Inn until noon tomorrow. If you change your mind, call." And he left.

"What was that all about?" I asked as we heard the new rental start up in the drive.

"He wants me to go back to Washington with him."

"He propose?"

"No. . . not exactly." Jewel grinned. "He isn't the marrying kind. But he's the 'living in sin' kind. What do you think? Can you see me as a 'significant other'?"

"Not exactly," I said, grinning back.

"Me either. Besides," she said, walking past me and heading for the kitchen. "Harmon's divorce will be final in a few months."

I heard the door to her bedroom off the kitchen close without my having said a word. Course, I figured it would be more fun to bring the whole thing up the next day at Dr. Marston's office.

THE UNDERGROUND STREAM

First Time in Paperback

VELDA JOHNSTON

AN OLD HOUSE WITH...EVEN OLDER SECRETS

For twenty-four years, Gail Loring has fought both her fear of the alcoholic haze in which the women of her family have lived *and* the haunting images of a man—her great-great-great-grandfather—called the Monster of Monroe Street.

Now Gail can run no longer. At her ancestral home in the summer resort town of Hampton Harbor, she vows to confront the past. She finds herself stepping back into the stream of time. She is Martha Fitzwilliam, a young wife and mother who lived here more than a hundred and fifty years ago. Gail shares Martha's secrets... and feels her terror. A terror she must pursue to its ultimate act of shattering violence....

"The vicissitudes of time and place are skillfully evoked in this eerie and often dream-like novel." —*Publishers Weekly*

A GINNY TRASK AND FRANK CARVER MYSTERY

COLD TRACKS

LEE WALLINGFORD

BLOOD LEAVES A DEADLY TRAIL

Tired of the violence of big-city crime, former narcotics agent
Frank Carver trades the streets of Seattle for the penny-ante stuff
of Oregon's Neskanie National Forest. Work is wonderfully, re-
freshingly dull for the forest's new law-enforcement officer. No
shootings. No bodies. No murders.

Until the corpse of Nino Alvarez, an immigrant worker, is found
in the woods by fire dispatcher Ginny Trask.

"Skillful debut. This intriguing pair of detectives—a burned-
out cop and a beautiful young widow—promise future en-
tertaining reading."

—*Publishers Weekly*

A DEB RALSTON MYSTERY

THE MENSA MURDERS

First Time In Paperback

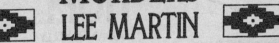

LEE MARTIN

DEAD BODIES LEAVE NO TRAILS....

Three women are murdered—in identical and very unusual ways.
The killer is solicitous—first breaking their necks, then tucking
them neatly into bed before cleaning the house and tending to the
pets.

With no trail to follow—since the killer insists on straightening up
the mess—Fort Worth detective Deb Ralston looks beyond the
scrubbed floors to discover the victims were all members of Mensa,
an organization for the superintelligent. Deb quickly discovers that
the group's members are not all as sane as they are smart.

"A believable sleuth in a superior series." —*Booklist*

First Time in Paperback

ELIZABETH TRAVIS

LOSERS WEEPERS

Hoping to acquire publishing rights to the final manuscript of recently deceased literary giant Charles Melton, Ben and Carrie Porter take a working vacation to his Riviera home. They're shocked to find the masterpiece in sections, each one bequeathed to a different heir. Whoever can collect the complete book will own the copyright—and be guaranteed a financially secure future.

Was Charles Melton an evil-minded scamp who set up this devilish scheme in the spirit of revenge? Or did he simply want all his heirs to reveal their true natures? When two of Melton's heirs are murdered, the Porters begin to suspect that a clever author had stuffed his final masterpiece with secrets—deadly secrets—which a killer intends to keep hidden at all costs.

Ben and Carrie are "two likeable, 30-something amateur sleuths."
—*Publishers Weekly*